Unexpected Development

Unexpected Development

Marlene Perez

A DEBORAH BRODIE BOOK
ROARING BROOK PRESS
BROOKFIELD, CONNECTICUT

Copyright © 2004 by Marlene Perez

A Deborah Brodie Book
Published by Roaring Brook Press
A Division of Holtzbrinck Publishing Holdings Limited Partnership
2 Old New Milford Road
Brookfield, Connecticut 06804

Library of Congress Cataloging-in-Publication Data
Perez, Marlene.
Unexpected Development/Marlene Perez.—1st ed.
p. cm.
"A Deborah Brodie Book."
Summary: In a series of papers for Honors English, a senior girl relates the difficul-
ties of being blessed with a voluptuous body that began appearing in fifth grade.
[1. Dating (Relationships)—Fiction. 2. Body image—Fiction. 3. Sex—Fiction.
4. High schools—Fiction. 5. Schools—Fiction.] I. Title.
PZ7.P4258Un 2004
[Fic]—dc22   200302173

ISBN 1-59643-006-0
2   4   6   8   10   9   7   5   3   1

Book design by Jennifer Browne
Printed in the United States of America

First edition

For Michael, Marissa, and Mikey
To the 6 a.m. weekend crews everywhere

Ann Hamilton, Linda Johns, and Terry Miller Shannon made this book possible with their wisdom, encouragement, and laughter. Many thanks to first readers Mary Pearson and Alex Uhl. Thanks also to Alex's staff at A Whale of a Tale. Thanks to my agent Steven Chudney. My dictionary does not contain enough superlatives for my editor, Deborah Brodie. Thank you, Deborah. Thanks to Vera and Jim Perez for the gift of time and the really great chair. Many thanks to my husband and children for putting up with me when I'm writing—and for putting up with me even more when I'm not.

Chapter
1

Mrs. Westland, I'm not sure you really want to get into what I did this summer. Sex, Mrs. Westland. The S word usually makes teachers turn pale and stutter. Sex is how I spent my summer vacation.

But what does "sex" really mean, anyway? Half the girls in this classroom have had sex, at least some form of it, but if you ask them, they're all virgins. It's all over but the penetration for most senior girls, but you wouldn't know to hear them tell it. Nobody mentions what happens when you're in love, though. What happens then?

You're probably getting all squirmy and uncomfortable right about now and wondering if you should call the guidance counselor or my parents.

Don't. It's too late. A done deal. And you did promise that whatever we wrote would stay confidential. Unless we wanted to "share our thoughts with the classroom."

I can't believe you assigned a topic like "How I Spent My Summer Vacation" for Honors English anyway. *Mrs. Westland, that was lame even when you were a kid.*

You waltzed into class on the first day, still smelling like suntan lotion. I can tell your heart is just not into school yet. I don't blame you. My heart's not really into it, either. After all, it is my senior year.

But I trust you, Mrs. Westland. I'll bet you don't even remember why I trust you, do you?

It was the start of my freshman year and even though they'd seen me every day of my life, nobody had figured out I was Dennis and David's younger sister. I registered about as much as the paint on the wall. Except for my most prominent features, which I'd tried to hide with one of David's huge shirts.

A senior named Peter Fenton had backed me into a corner, making rude comments about my breasts. He pinned me against the barf green wall. With one hand, he locked both my wrists in his meaty paw. I didn't know what to do. What he would do.

I looked for help from two girls I thought were my friends. Their eyes gleamed with nervous excitement.

They watched and giggled as he unbuttoned the top button of my shirt. I writhed, trying to get away, but I was like a butterfly stuck on a pin. Peter laughed. He knew no one would stop him. He popped a second button free.

But that's as far as he got.

Because you came to my rescue, Mrs. Westland.

"Mr. Fenton"—your voice was like the low roar of a rushing river—"if you do not release that young woman immediately, I will make sure you are benched for the entire basketball season."

Peter tried the cute-kid-caught-in-the-cookie-jar look, but since he had his hands in my particular cookie jar, you weren't having any of it. "And why don't you go tell Coach Simms your after-school schedule is booked for the next week or two. In detention."

I watched Peter's face fall, and then he was the butterfly on a pin.

You came over to me and gently buttoned up my buttons and told me to go wash my face. As I left, I saw you corner my no-longer-snickering friends. Make that ex-friends.

I avoided Peter for my entire freshman year. I couldn't tell Dennis and David. I was too embarrassed. And it helped that you told Coach Simms that his star player would not be playing at all that season if he didn't leave me alone. Then Peter graduated and left Iowa. He drifted back into Fairview this summer, along with ominous whispers of where he'd been.

I really do trust you, Mrs. Westland.

And you should trust me, I don't think this is something to share with the world. Someone once told me that love is a strange thing. He was right, more so than even he knew. I learned that love is strange and wild and sometimes even frightening. I'm not sure if the rest of the world would understand what happened this summer. But I think you will.

It all began in June, when I got a job at the Pancake Palace, the restaurant my best friend Jilly's dad owns.

I was sitting at the kitchen table eating a peach from our tree when Dad walked in.

"Megan, no school today?"

"High school got out last week, Dad."

My brothers Dennis and David were in your class last year, so you probably appreciate my dad's usual state of bewilderment. They're only a year older than me, but a lot wilder. Dennis is the ringleader, but I'm betting you remember. Most people do.

My mom hasn't exactly been tuning in for today's episode since she had Dillon and Dakota. Yep, not one, but two sets of twin boys in my family. And they're sixteen years apart.

"Oh." Dad tried to cover, but I could see he was surprised. He taught at the junior high, and it was in session for another week.

"What's on tap for this afternoon then?" Dad is big on using time wisely, which is why my big brothers were nowhere in sight.

"Work. Remember? My new job." Dad's face was blank.

"Pancake Palace." Another *oh* in response.

"Want to take your car?" Dad picked up my abandoned car

keys and jangled them. Omigod, I couldn't be seen in that monstrosity.

"Uh, I can't, Dad. Jilly's on her way over to pick me up for work. She'll be here any minute. Remember, I'm spending the night?"

Dad apologized. "I know it's not much, but it's the best your mother and I could do."

"It's okay, Dad, really."

"The new shop teacher, Mr. Blake, is going to help me fix up your car."

"Thanks, Dad. I like the car. I really do. I'm running late, that's all." I kissed him on the forehead. "I'll take it for a drive tomorrow, okay?"

My car is the ugliest thing I've ever seen. It looks like it was patched together by a mad mechanic. The Frankenstein's monster of American-made cars.

Dad can't help it that he hadn't had a raise in forever. Like the fifteen years we've lived here. Okay, it probably only *seems* like Dad's never had a raise. You're a teacher, so you know what they pay you people. You try feeding a family of seven on a teacher's wages. Dennis and David both got football scholarships, or they'd be attending the local community college.

You've lived in Fairview only a few years, so maybe you haven't noticed: Church is *it* in our town. If you don't pray, you don't stay. Everyone in town attends church regularly, which means Wednesday nights and Sundays. With the exception of my family, that is.

My parents don't believe in organized religion, so we're the only family in the entire town that doesn't go to church. Maybe that's why I feel like I don't fit in with the rest of Fairview. Because Dennis and David play football, which is the town's other religion, and Dad won some big-deal teaching award when I was little, my family's not exactly blackballed. But sometimes, I'm not sure I fit in anywhere in the entire state of Iowa.

I went to my room and changed for work. I changed into my work bra, an item that was the bra version of an armored tank, and about as comfortable. The box promised minimization and containment, but then again, so do certain medieval instruments of torture.

My job at the pancake house was one of the better jobs in town, since there would be, presumably, lots of tips. And a bunch of my friends worked there, too, including my neighbor Susi Fielding. Susi, Jilly, and I used to be best friends, but ever since her dad remarried and moved to Des Moines, Susi spends her time with boys. Lots of boys.

Jilly got me the job. Mr. Henderson, her dad, owns the restaurant, along with most of the town. You'd think we'd get the best shifts, but Mr. Cooper, the manager, hated us both equally. He thought we were spying for Mr. Henderson or something.

I looked in the mirror again. Who in the world thought head-to-toe red and purple was flattering? Too bad the uniform was so ugly. I made a face in the mirror.

It wasn't fair, either. Only the waiters and waitresses had to wear purple polyester. The cooks and dishwashers got to wear brown cotton pants with white chef's coats.

I resembled a purple lightbulb. If you haven't noticed, I'm what polite people call top-heavy. You don't even want to think about what the impolite say. *Nice rack*, usually.

If you're wondering where I get my ideas, it's from Dennis and David. The girls they date would die if they heard the way my brothers talk about them.

Jilly says I need to be a little more trusting of the male species, but with brothers like mine, who can blame me? And let's not forget my charming ex-boyfriend, Sam. And she should talk—when her dad left her mom, Jilly fell apart. She sticks to her boyfriend, Lyle, like glue.

This summer, I saw the best and the worst in them. Guys, I mean. I went over to the wall where I'd hung a huge poster board. It was covered with magazine cutouts of every model I'd like to resemble. None of them had chests to speak of. Dennis and David would never let me hear the end of it if they knew the real reason I spent my days cutting and pasting.

I stood sideways in front of the mirror and sighed. Nope, my chest hadn't miraculously dissolved or deflated or anything. Sometimes, I can actually convince myself, for a minute or so, that I'm pretty, that I'm smart. That someone would be interested in me for me, instead of these five-pound mounds.

Can you believe I know over twenty words for breasts? Probably more, if you count the ones I'm too embarrassed to repeat. I started collecting them along with the stares and comments I received when I developed unexpectedly in fifth grade.

Someday I'm going to take care of these lumps. I've been saving for years to get rid of them. Right now, I have to choose between a boob reduction and college. If I don't get a scholarship, I'll have an aching back and gouging bra straps a few years longer.

The day after the end of my junior year, I called a doctor's office in Des Moines. I wasn't dumb enough to have it done locally. Besides, it wasn't like there were plastic surgeons on every corner in Fairview, Iowa. I checked the date circled in purple on my calendar. Six weeks to go before my consultation with the cosmetic surgeon.

I found some clothes to change into after work and stuffed them into a bag, along with some fashion magazines and my chem book. I knew I'd be waiting for Jilly. I carried my gear into the hallway to wait for my ride.

My feet bumped up against blocks, toy cars, a basketball, and a fungus-growing pile of Dakota and Dillon's clothes. Mom's too involved with a second round of playdates and preschool to actually clean on a regular basis.

Honk! Honk! Jilly was laying on her horn. On my way out the door, I almost plowed into Mom, who was back from a playdate and carried a twin on each hip. As usual, she looked like a porcelain doll lugging around two fullbacks.

She inspected me briefly. "Stand up straight, Megan."

I felt myself slouching even more. I'm pretty sure my tiny mother wonders how she got a daughter with breasts the size of naval torpedoes. Straight posture doesn't do anything but draw eyes to the critical spot.

"Jilly's home alone again. I won't be home tonight. Dad already said it was okay." I flung the words at her retreating back. But she was already in the kitchen.

"Bye, Mom. You have a nice night, too," I said. My mom doesn't care what I do as long as boys aren't involved. Most of the time, I don't think she even remembers she has a daughter. But if a guy gets within fifty feet of me, she acts like she's the only thing keeping me from sinking into a life of sexual depravity.

You should have seen her when I was dating Sam. She practically told me that a boy like Sam only wanted one thing from a girl like me. Whatever "a girl like me" means. I thought my mother, who loves me, or claims to, anyway, would have a little more faith in her own daughter. At least my job gets me out of her hair, and so far, Mom hasn't checked up on me at the Palace.

If you have better taste than most of the people in town,

then you might not be familiar with it, but Pancake Palace is that ugly place off the interstate. You know the one, with the giant statue of a chubby king.

Mr. Henderson has to be color-blind. Why else would you dress a statue like a Technicolor nightmare? If you press a button on the statue, the king says stuff like, "We'll give you the royal treatment at the Pancake Palace." The entire restaurant is in the ever-popular purple-and-red color scheme.

It used to be a plain old cafe called Ruth's. Then Mr. Henderson bought it and let Jilly's new stepmom decorate it. If Barbie were a prostitute, it would be her dream home. Stephanie even named each room of the restaurant after royal homes: the Buckingham, the Windsor, and the Balmoral.

Friday nights were always slow. People usually headed to Ames, the college town a few miles away. The manager always made Jilly stay late, slow or not. He always made me, the person who really needed the money, punch out early.

I tossed my bag into the backseat. Jilly pointed her chin at my car and shuddered.

"What is that?" She tossed her blond hair away from her face and let out a scream of laughter.

"Shh, my dad will hear. You know what it is, it's my car."

"That's a car?" she said. "That's not a car, that's a-a Beast."

"Come on, Jillian, be nice. We don't all get red convertibles for our sixteenth birthday."

"At least your parents stayed home on your birthday."

The quaver in Jilly's voice got to me. I wouldn't take Jilly's parents for all the shiny sports cars on the lot. My mom drove me crazy, but at least we were in the same zip code most of the time.

I reached over and gave her a half shove/half hug. The kind you give your best friend to say "I love you" and "knock it the hell off."

"The Beast it is." I jumped out of the car and went over to my pathetic ride, brandishing an imaginary champagne bottle. "I dub thee the Beast."

I hopped back into Jilly's car, happy to see her laughing.

"Let's go or we'll be late," I said, as I reached for the radio dial. Music never fails to cheer up Jilly.

Her mood shifted, and she gave me an impish smile as she cranked the volume and pointed the car in the general direction of the Pancake Palace.

Jilly's shift started before mine, so I sat in the break room and read a magazine while I waited to punch in. I was reading an article on luscious lip-glosses when a voice interrupted.

"Hi, Megan, how are you?"

There was the smiling face of Jake Darrow, love of my life and a totally taken, just-graduated senior. He was most often summed up in one word: Yum! His chef's jacket didn't detract from his good looks one bit.

His eyes are brown and make me feel warm and sweet, like maple syrup injected into my veins. Jake is also the nicest guy around, almost too good to be true. He's also a good friend of my brothers'.

"Hi, you work here?" I replied with sparkling wit. *Like, why else is he dressed up like a chef, Megan? It's not Halloween.*

"For the summer," he said. "I need money for college."

As I stared at him, my magazine fell onto the floor. "HOW TO GET THE GUY OF YOUR DREAMS," the title screamed. How's that for ironic? He stood right in front of me.

Jake bent down to pick up my magazine. I was desperate for a witty remark. I could only stare in complete stupefaction as he handed my magazine back.

I've had a crush on Jake since seventh grade. The first thing I noticed was the way he said my name. I fell for him, literally, in 7th/8th P.E. We were playing table tennis or dodgeball or something.

I twisted my ankle and fell on top of him. He asked, "Megan, are you okay?" in a voice of chocolate velvet, laced with real concern. My heart hasn't been the same since.

That same year, Savannah Robins moved to Fairview, and Jake was officially off the market. They both graduated this year, steady as ever. Everyone predicts a blissful wedded future for them. You know, they were voted Couple Least Likely to Be Cheating on Each Other in 10 Years, or something.

The silence was getting awkward. As I opened my mouth to spew out some inane comment, Jake said, "Well, I'd better get to work. I guess I'll see you around."

Fifteen minutes later, I punched in. I had to greet and seat a few senior citizens coming for the early-bird special. Then Peter Fenton came in and sat down in my section.

Before I could even ask, Jilly slapped a menu in his hand and stood there until he ordered. Jilly is the best. I mouthed a thank-you to her and bussed three of her tables. I would have bussed a hundred of the grimiest, kid-infested tables just to avoid Peter Fenton.

I almost collided with Jake when I took the bus tubs back to the dishwasher. I'm sure the heat and steam were what made me flush. At least, I hope *he* thought so.

As soon as I got the chance, I was going to corner Jilly and make her spill anything she knew about Jake. He lived just a few doors down from her.

Then about ten tables walked in at once, and I didn't have time to breathe, let alone obsess over Jake. Finally, the supper rush died down. I hadn't seen the slime leave, but Peter was gone, thankfully. Jilly stood in the waitress station filing her nails and getting the evil eye from Mr. Cooper.

There was hardly a soul left in the place, so I made myself appear busy by filling already-full ketchup bottles. Mr. Cooper's wife called to nag, so he hurried to the back office to take his licking. I immediately headed for Jilly.

"When did Jake start working here?" I hissed.

"My God, Megan, haven't you got over him yet?" She practically announced it over the intercom.

"Shhh! Keep your voice down! He's working tonight." I pulled a small mirror from my uniform pocket and twitched my curls this way and that, trying to make my hair behave for once. Mr. Cooper made us scrape every strand of hair into a tight bun, but my hair never cooperates.

"Look at you. I knew it. If I had told you ahead of time, you'd have acted like a spaz for days. Jake is nothing to get all amped up about."

With a feeling of dread, as the last words left her mouth, I felt someone move up behind me. Please, please, don't let it be Jake.

"It's slow tonight, huh?" It was Jake.

I shot Jilly a look. The I'll-kill-you-if-he-heard-you look. She mouthed a sorry to me. Thankfully, Jake hadn't heard anything. Or at least he acted like he hadn't heard anything.

We were practically the only ones in the restaurant. Mr. Cooper was still in his office being chewed out by his wife. A regular sat at the counter, nursing a cup of coffee.

"Friday nights are always slow. It's date night. Why aren't you out with Savannah tonight?" she said.

I pictured her face, flattened.

"She's in Phoenix, visiting her grandmother. She won't be back until right before we leave for college."

Mr. Cooper came out of the office. His face was red. Now was not the time to be seen standing around. I turned around to fill salt and pepper shakers, while Jilly grabbed a rag and halfheartedly swiped down the microwave.

Jake didn't seem worried, though. "Slow night tonight, boss. Mind if I take off?"

"Well, I guess it's okay. We close in an hour anyway." Mr. Cooper sounded almost human.

"Megan, go ahead and punch out. Jillian will close," he added.

"But Mr. Cooper, I'm supposed to close tonight," I protested. I knew it wouldn't do any good. Mr. Cooper was a sadist.

He probably thought Jilly had a date with Lyle or something, but I was spending the night at Jilly's. She hated staying in that big house all alone.

Jilly also hated working in her father's restaurant, mostly because he didn't give her a choice about it. She would rather babysit Dakota and Dillon than work at the Palace. I know, because she tried.

"I said, Jillian will close, Megan. Do you understand me?" I understand what an asshole you are, I thought. As usual, I waited in the back room for Jilly and helped her with whatever closing tasks I could without getting caught.

I punched out and changed in the employee bathroom. We had talked about riding around after we closed, so I put on my favorite green shirt and a pair of jeans. I even put on a little mascara and blush, something I rarely did.

When I came out, Jake was sitting at the break table. He got up and grabbed a gym bag. No one ever wore a Palace uniform after work.

It's Friday night, he's probably got a date, I thought, but then remembered Savannah was out of town. I grabbed a soda and sat down. Jilly had at least another hour before she could leave. I'd already finished reading my *Cosmo Girl*.

I had some chemistry reading to do, but I didn't want to advertise I was taking a college course over the summer. That left staring at the clock and waiting, something I'm not very good at.

I thought I saw Jake walk out as I checked my watch. He wore a deep blue shirt and shorts. Without saying good-bye, he walked toward the front. It took me by surprise. Jake had always been polite.

I sometimes even thought he liked me in that I've-already-got-a-girlfriend-but-you're-cute way. Why did I get my hopes up whenever I saw him? I couldn't even talk to him without sounding like a total idiot.

It was driving me crazy watching the clock, and I finally gave up and dug out my chemistry book. Geeky image or not, I needed something to do.

Jake came back with a soda and an order of fries and sat next to me. So close I could see the freckles on his cheek.

"Want some?" he offered.

"No, thanks."

He dipped a fry into a mound of ketchup.

"You look different. Good, I mean."

"Thanks. It's probably because I'm out of that hideous polyester nightmare they call a uniform." I laughed, but forced myself to shut up fast. My brothers say when I laugh I sound like a pig snorting.

Jake laughed, too, a soft, sexy chuckle. We sat in silence again, but this time I didn't feel like I had ants in my undies. "You sure you don't want a fry?"

"Why not?" I took one and blew on it to cool it. I caught Jake staring at my lips. He didn't say anything. He didn't have to. One look and I melted like butter.

He turned my book over. "Studying? Chemistry, even. Dennis and David are pretty proud of you, you know," Jake said.

"Proud of me? When?" I couldn't keep the surprise from my voice.

"Well, for example, when you made National Honor Society," he replied.

"Jake, you remember that?" I said.

"Hey, I've got to take off," he said. "Are you working tomorrow?"

"Yeah. Mr. Cooper has no mercy. Jilly and I are on for the six a.m. shift. How about you?"

"We get to work together then. See you tomorrow." He got up to leave, then hesitated.

"Do you need a ride?" Jake asked.

"That's okay. I'm staying at Jilly's tonight."

"I could drop you off so you wouldn't have to hang around waiting. It's on my way."

I didn't bother to act surprised. I knew they were neighbors, but so did everyone else in town.

"Okay. Thanks. Let me tell Jilly." I couldn't believe I was doing this.

"I can't believe you're doing this," Jilly whispered, when I motioned her over to get her house keys. "Will you be okay alone with him?"

"He's a friend of my brothers'. It's just a ride home. That's it."

"Be careful, okay? I see that look in your eyes. I just don't want you to get hurt."

Jake appeared just after Jilly ended her sentence. She gave me a hug, and managed to whisper in my ear before I left.

Her "remember he's taken" echoed in my head all the way to the car.

Chapter

2

Mrs. Westland, when we left the restaurant, I felt like someone was watching me. It was probably just a guilty conscience. I wasn't doing anything wrong and neither was Jake.

Jake put his hand on the small of my back, as he opened the car door for me. As it opened, a wall of perfume hit me like a slap. Savannah's perfume. I couldn't help but recognize the scent she wore. You could smell her coming down the halls at school. I didn't see how he could hang out with Savannah without a gas mask.

Jake had opened the passenger door with the ease of long habit. Savannah had him well trained. He didn't even act self-conscious, like most guys would have.

I must have wrinkled my nose, because Jake smiled a little. "Savannah's perfume takes some getting used to." Then he looked away, like he wished he hadn't said anything.

It didn't take long to get to Jilly's. We didn't exactly live in a metropolis.

The Henderson house was this Rhett-and-Scarlett *Gone with the Wind* monstrosity that sat on a hill above the golf course. The house is beautiful and a little ridiculous, too. Like a woman who wears a cocktail dress to shop for groceries. The neighboring bungalows and old farmhouses seemed to draw up the skirts of their porches in disgust at such flamboyance.

Mrs. Westland, I was so nervous during the drive that I talked nonstop about absolutely nothing. Jake mostly listened. He acted like he had something on his mind. As he turned into the driveway, he asked about Sam, my ex-boyfriend. There was an awkward pause.

"We haven't been going out since spring break," I said.

I wondered why he wanted to know. Sam had told me that long-distance relationships never worked, and then he dumped me. A few months later, I found out he'd met someone at a freshman mixer. I kind of expected it. I was still in high school and he was in college. It was such a cliché.

Right after the breakup, Butterball Belling told me the news about Sam's new girlfriend. It was her pleasure, believe me when I tell you this. What she didn't know is that I'd been expecting it.

Jake parked and cut the engine. He got out to open my door. I bet the oh-so- perfect Savannah takes him for granted.

"Thanks for the ride, Jake." I grabbed my bag and bolted

from the car. The street was deserted, thank god. Butterball Belling was Jilly's neighbor and the biggest gossip in our class. I hoped she wouldn't be home.

If it got back to Savannah that Jake gave me a ride home, I was dead. She had graduated, but there were still plenty of her viciously perky buddies left in school. They'd gladly make my life miserable just because I got a ride home from Savannah's man.

My escape was short-lived. Jake cut me off at the pass and strolled up the walk with me, walking as slow as honey dripping. Why was he walking so slowly?

The motion sensor lights of the house went on, just as Jake reached for me. It was like we were standing in a spotlight. I jumped about a mile, thinking Jake was going to try to cop a feel or something. It's not that I'm conceited. It's just that some guys will try stuff with girls—girls with big boobs especially.

All my breasts ever meant to me were problems. Personally, I didn't see the attraction. Why do guys turn into drooling idiots at the sight of mammary glands, even mine, which are mostly concealed underneath the baggy sweaters I wear? I didn't fool myself that they were interested in me. I didn't think Jake was that kind of guy, though.

Turns out he wasn't. He was only trying to take the key from me to unlock the door. I really wasn't used to all that gentlemanly stuff. When I dated Sam, his idea of a romantic date was a round of miniature golf with his drunken buddies and their obnoxious girlfriends.

Jake opened the door for me and I practically fell in. Grace under pressure, that's me. I felt foolish, so I did something I knew I'd end up regretting. "Want to come in for a beer?"

Oh, boy, Megan, I told myself, Jilly will never let you hear the end of it if she gets home and Jake's here. She wasn't trying to run my life. She just looked out for me. Even when I wanted to do stupid stuff like invite Jake in for a beer.

"Sure. It's still a little early to go home." Jake surprised me. Despite all the times he hung out with my brothers, we'd never spent more than a few minutes alone.

We walked through the Hendersons' spotless white living room. We weren't allowed to even sit down in that room.

He whistled and then said, "Nice place, but it reminds me of a museum."

"Jilly's mom had it redecorated by some big-name designer right before the divorce. Stephanie, Jilly's step-monster, likes to drop his name everywhere, so she didn't have the place redone. We mostly hang out in the basement."

There were basement steps right off the living room. I flicked on the hall light and Jake followed me down the curved staircase.

The basement wasn't what most people think of when they hear the word "basement." Besides a couple of extra bedrooms, there was a huge family room with a big-screen television and a full bar.

Mr. Henderson had a fit if any of the hard liquor was gone, but he never said a thing if a few beers went missing. Which they frequently did. Stephanie was usually so full of scotch and soda, she never noticed.

We practically lived in the basement. The rest of the house was pretty much off-limits. Stephanie was neat for a drunk— she even badgered the maid if the thick carpeting wasn't vac-uumed a couple of times every day.

I went to the bar's fridge and pulled out a couple of beers. Jake sat on the couch. I handed him a bottle and sat in a chair. My stomach was doing cartwheels just being alone in the same room with him.

"Jilly's parents aren't around much, I guess." Jake leaned back on the leather sofa. God, his legs were long and muscular.

"No, but I'm over here a lot, especially since my mom's hav-ing a fit right now getting the twins ready for college." My older brothers were in the same class as Jake. Best friends, in fact. I would die if my tormenting older brothers found out I had a thing for Jake. I'd never hear the end of it.

"Yeah, my mom, too." Jake changed the subject. "I heard Jilly and Lyle are practically engaged."

Lyle is Jilly's boyfriend. Blond, tan, and gorgeous. Her per-fect Ken-doll boyfriend. He waits in his toy box till she's ready to take him out and play with him again. He goes right back in without a fuss. But I'm wondering what it's going to be like for her when they're married. You can't exactly put your husband in a toy box, now can you?

"Not practically engaged, they are engaged. They're getting married next summer. Right after we graduate."

Jake studied me a moment. "You don't sound very happy about it."

Boy, I was doing a lousy job of keeping my mouth shut tonight. I took a sip of my beer to give myself time to think.

"Well, Jilly and I had always planned on getting out of Iowa after high school. Maybe move to Minneapolis or even L.A. Now her dad is buying them a house in town. They're moving in right after they get married."

"I'm going to college on the West Coast. Stanford."

"I know," I said quickly. Too quickly. "Dennis told me," I added.

I squirmed. My bra was digging into my flesh. I couldn't wait to take the darned thing off.

"What about you? Do you know where you're going to go after you graduate?" Jake seemed interested.

"I'm applying to a couple of different colleges. The one I really want to attend is—kind of expensive for my folks. They'll have three kids in college at the same time. I need to make as much money as possible, but you saw how Mr. Cooper is."

"He can be a jerk sometimes, but he's not too bad after you get to know him. We go to the same church."

I did some mental eye rolling. Of course they did. Which maybe explained why Mr. Cooper went easy on him tonight.

"Everyone in town knows his wife is driving him crazy right now."

I figured he'd heard his parents talking about it. It wasn't exactly a secret around the restaurant, either. Everyone knew to stay out of Mr. Cooper's way after he'd been talking to his wife. I didn't want to talk about Mr. Cooper anymore.

"Love is a strange thing." There was a peculiar note in Jake's voice.

"Yeah, love sucks most of the time," I replied.

"So, I guess you're not serious about anyone right now?" Jake asked. "You didn't have any plans for tonight or anything."

Hey, what was this? He made me sound like a total loser who couldn't get a date on a bet.

I glared at him. "I prefer to stay away from anything serious till I get to college. I can't imagine anything worse than dating the same person all through high school." Oops.

Jake glared back for a minute. Then we both cracked up. He got a weird expression on his face and said, "I wish more people felt the way you do."

I wanted to ask about him and Savannah, but couldn't work up the nerve.

"I always thought you were too good for Sam, you know," Jake said. "There are probably lots of guys who want to ask you out."

"What makes you think that?" What I really wanted to know is since when had Jake Darrow been paying attention to my love life?

"I mean, you're smart, funny, and cute," Jake said. "Lots of guys must ask you out."

My heart did a little dance. Jake thought I was cute.

"Dennis and David are my older brothers," I said.

"Point taken." Jake and I shared a smile. Dennis loved to torment my would-be boyfriends. I'm still not sure why Sam stuck around as long as he did.

He studied his beer for a minute. "Do you mind if I ask you something kind of personal?"

My heart beat hard. What was he going to ask?

"Why did you and Sam break up? Was he unfaithful?"

I opened my mouth, but no sound came out.

Jake leaned in closer.

I nodded. I choked out the words: "I acted like it didn't matter, but it did. If he'd only just told me . . ."

Then Jake Darrow said something I never expected to hear.

"I've been unfaithful," he said, "at least mentally." He took a deep breath. "Actually, I've been wanting to talk to you about this. I've been thinking about someone and I can't get her out of my mind. I told Savannah—"

A slamming door cut Jake off from whatever he was going to say. A minute later, Jilly hollered from upstairs, "Megan, I'm home. Where are you?"

It was amazing the noise a skinny thing like Jilly could make. She sounded like a herd of pissed-off elephants. She stomped and paused in an obvious way, stopping to call my name every few minutes.

We looked at each other and laughed. "What does she think we could be doing?" Jake whispered.

"Well, we have been unchaperoned for"—I checked my watch—"a total of forty-five minutes, including the drive home."

"She has a dirty mind," Jake said. "Let's mess with her a little."

We hid in the downstairs closet, the two of us wedged in with Mr. Henderson's golf clubs and a couple of winter coats. Jake left the door open a crack so we could watch her reaction. She flew down the stairs in a total tizzy. We choked back our laughter.

"Megan, Jake! Where are you guys?"

In the closet, I felt like hyperventilating. It wasn't so funny anymore. In fact, it seemed positively dangerous. Jake and I stood face-to-face, pressed up against each other like sardines in a can. I was pretty sure, though, that most sardines weren't cursed with breasts the size of small hams.

He was so close I couldn't think. I just inhaled the smell of him. He smelled like temptation and Ivory soap.

I leaned as far away as I could, but my breasts still brushed up against his chest and our knees bumped repeatedly. I forgot to breathe, and prayed Jilly would find us before I made a fool of myself and lunged at Jake.

Jilly searched for us in the family room. I thought she'd see our beers and figure it out. She walked down the hall and stopped by our hiding spot in the closet. Passing by the closet, she went straight to one of the bedrooms.

For a minute, I thought about what it would be like to be in that bedroom with Jake. It made my blood bubble up like hot oil. The door must have been shut, because I heard her knock softly.

"She does have a dirty mind," I said under my breath. "Thanks a lot, Jilly."

I couldn't believe it. My best friend thought I was a total hose-bag. I ignored the nagging feeling that I might be. For the right guy. For Jake. I glanced over at him guiltily, but I couldn't see much in the dark. When she didn't get an answer, I heard the door creak open.

"Where are you guys?" She sounded puzzled. She passed by the closet, and after we heard her go by, Jake opened the closet door very quietly. We stepped out and hollered, "Boo!"

She let out a little scream and jumped about a mile. When she saw it was us, she relaxed. She laughed and then said, "Jeez, you scared me!"

Jilly chatted away, but not before her eyes scanned me head-to-toe. Inspecting me for love rumples, probably. I guess she could tell I hadn't been up to anything. It's a good thing my best friend can't always read my mind.

Chapter

3

Mrs. Westland, did you think that maybe Jake sneaked a kiss goodnight? No chance of that. Jilly chaperoned from the front porch while I walked Jake to his car. I was a little relieved. I wasn't sure my nervous system could handle any more alone time with Jake Darrow.

Jilly and I went back in and popped a bag of popcorn in the microwave. We took it to her room to watch a movie. She has cable, even the premium channels. When I spend the night, we stay up late and watch old movies. Lyle calls it our movie-of-the-week night.

I threw myself on her bed. "Jilly, what do you think about the way I look?"

"Is this about Jake?"

"No, this is about me. Am I—deformed?"

Jilly choked on a popcorn kernel. "God, no! You're beautiful. And you've got a great body."

"You mean these?" I pointed to my chest.

"No, I mean the whole package, Megan. You've got long legs, a flat stomach. If you'd just stop hiding behind all those baggy clothes you wear."

"I don't always wear baggy clothes."

"Ninety-nine percent of the time, you look like you're wearing David's hand-me-downs."

I must have looked guilty.

"I knew it!" Jilly said. "I can't believe you actually wear your brothers' clothes."

"It helps hide, you know—" I gestured in the general area of my chest.

"What's wrong with having breasts? I'd kill for your shape, or any shape at all." Jilly's an A-cup. I knew it bothered her, just like she knew being a D-cup bothered me.

"You're perfect, blond, slender, and guys love you."

"I'm skinny. And guys flirt because I'm safe. Everyone knows I'd never break up with Lyle." It was true. Jilly was loyal through and through.

"I bet guys don't say rude things about your breasts."

"Oh no? What about 'flat as a board'?"

"What about 'bodacious set of ta-tas'? I cringe every time they show *An Officer and a Gentleman* on late-night TV," I said.

"What about 'You're so flat, the walls are jealous'? *Degrassi Junior High*." Jilly topped me, as usual.

We've been having our quote contests for years. It's silly, but it always makes me feel better. Jilly wins every time, but then, she spent a lot of time alone with the TV.

"Okay, okay. Neither of us has it better than the other. And speaking of movies, let's watch one," I said.

I clicked on the TV, and we watched a movie in our pj's. I didn't feel like going out, and we both had to be up early. She fell asleep halfway through the love scene. I guess you didn't need to watch it when you lived it every day. I clicked off the TV as the credits rolled, but couldn't fall asleep.

I didn't know what Jilly was so uptight about. We'd been friends since preschool and she always looked out for me, but this was extreme for her. I'd had a crush on Jake since time began, but so what? He had never even dated anyone else since he started seeing Savannah. Believe me, in a town the size of Fairview, I'd have known.

Savannah is a bird-boned beauty with big brown eyes and brown hair. She also has rosy skin and two tiny dimples. She barely has a chest and her hips are small enough for Jake to span with his two hands. I should know, I'd watched him do it enough times.

I'm Savannah's complete opposite. I have enough breasts and hips for both of us. If Savannah was Jake's type, and she apparently was, then what was I? He probably thought of me as the twins' kid sister, if he thought of me at all.

Dating a guy like Jake would drive me nuts anyway. He's funny, sweet, and gorgeous. Girls chase after him by the carload. I don't think my ego could take it. Everyone would assume that Jake was dating me for one reason—make that two reasons. And I'd be afraid they were right.

I punched the pillow and rolled over to set the alarm. Why couldn't I be happy with someone like Brent Swenson? He'd been following me around like a puppy for the last few weeks.

He kept asking me out, but every time he'd called, I'd had to work. Or something. Instead, I turn to Jell-O over a guy like Jake, who's so taken he practically has a ring in his nose for Savannah to lead him around with.

I went upstairs to the library. The Hendersons never set foot in there, but it was fully stocked with all the bestsellers. I found a book but couldn't get into it.

There were some scissors in the junk drawer in the kitchen. I grabbed them and found the magazines still in my bag. I slid them out and snipped perfect bodies until I was calm enough to sleep.

The alarm rang way too early the next morning. We both had the six a.m. shift but Jilly got up first. She likes to primp. It wasn't like I had to wait for her to finish in the shower or anything; there are five bathrooms in her house. For three people. Most of the time, Stephanie and Mr. Henderson weren't even home. Jilly and I rattle around that house like two pennies in a glass jar.

The ex-Mrs. Henderson, Jilly's mom, was currently on the West Coast. She told everyone she was visiting a spa and enjoying the proceeds from the divorce settlement, but Jilly thought she was getting a little nip-and-tuck while she was there. She must have been getting a major overhaul, as long as she'd been gone.

I yawned and stretched. As brutal as it was to get out of bed in the morning, I had to get ready. I might as well spend some time applying a little makeup. Of course it wasn't because I thought I'd see Jake.

We got to work with about a minute to spare. Of course, I checked to see if Jake was working the minute we walked in.

Jilly caught me. "Your heartthrob isn't here, Megan."

"Like I care." Tough comeback, but in reality, my heart sank.

Moldy Dave waved cheerfully at us, and then turned to flip something at the grill. Moldy Dave's real name is Jim Moldave, but everyone calls him Moldy Dave.

He has this strange fascination with gross stuff—mold, vomit, road kill. He calls it scientific interest. I call it sick. He was my science partner sophomore year, when we dissected frogs. Moldy Dave's eyes gleamed as he precisely sliced into our specimen. I thought of Kermit, my childhood favorite from *Sesame Street*, singing "It's Not Easy Being Green." I spent the entire time trying not to throw up. On the upside, we both got an A.

I can never figure out why the locals don't just turn around and drive the ten miles to McDonald's when they see Moldy

Dave standing in the kitchen. They have to see him. The chef's window is practically the first thing you see when you walk in.

Besides, Moldy Dave is hard to miss. He's six foot six with this huge beaky nose and platinum hair. There's something not quite fully formed about him, like a baby vulture fresh from the egg.

Jilly went to punch in, still yawning. A minute later, she came back to where I was standing. She waved around a piece of paper. "Mr. Cooper is starting a softball team for the restaurant."

"I have class." I hate all competitive sports.

Jilly said, "Your class is on Tuesday and Thursday mornings."

"So?" I said.

"So you can still make it to the games. It'll be fun. Let's join," Jilly said.

"What'll be fun?" I hadn't seen Jake walk up. My heart did a little flip as he peered over my shoulder.

"A summer softball team for the restaurant. Let's all sign up," Jilly said.

I hesitated. I had played ball with the twins when we were little. I was a pretty good pitcher. I used to strike Dennis and David out all the time. Until I developed breasts.

Mrs. Westland, I don't know if you've noticed, but my breasts get in the way of everything. Most girls don't even want to be friends with me. They're afraid these useless things will lure their loser boyfriends away. As if.

Not Jilly, though. She's totally secure and she hardly ever asks me for anything. What could it hurt? And there was the added Jake bonus. Jilly signed her name with a flourish.

Jake added his name and held the pen out to me. "It will be fun, I promise."

"Okay, okay." I signed my name, and then groaned. "The first practice is right after work today."

For the next few hours, we served a mountain of pancakes. My stomach churned like a blender every time I caught sight of Jake's broad shoulders.

After Jilly and I punched out, she dropped me off at home to change. I told her I'd drive the Beast to the field and meet her there.

When I pulled up, Jilly was sitting in her car, top down, radio blaring, swaying to the beat. We walked over to the practice diamond. No Jake in sight.

He *said* he'd see us there. He was giving Moldy Dave a ride. I tried to ignore the excitement thrumming through my veins at the thought of seeing Jake again.

"Who's the coach?" I said to Jilly. We'd never thought to check.

"I hope it's not Mr. Cooper."

The coach was Mr. Cooper. He stood in the middle of the field, wearing a bright purple T-shirt that read *Pancake Palace Royals* in red letters. He held a clipboard and had a bossy little whistle draped around his neck. He bellowed out rapid-fire instructions at a couple of kids from the restaurant. They ran around the bases with perplexed looks. Mr. C. turned and shouted instructions to the next group of poor fools.

Susi Fielding stood in the outfield, snapping her bubble gum and looking bored. She wore butt-cut shorts and a halter top. I felt overdressed in a huge tee of David's and an old pair of shorts. I couldn't imagine myself in a halter top, ever, but especially not to play softball. As it was, I had on my extra-strength sports bra just to minimize the bounce potential.

Mr. Cooper hadn't acknowledged our arrival yet, so I walked to the outfield. I liked Susi, even though she dressed like a hoochie mama sometimes.

"Hi, Susi. What's up?"

"Hi, Megan. We're doing drills."

"Drills? I thought this was supposed to be for fun."

"That was before Mr. C. heard about the tri-county restaurant championship."

I walked back to where Jilly had planted herself on the bleachers.

"Bad news, Jilly, competitive sports." We both shuddered.

"You don't know how bad this is. Once Mr. Cooper got in a competition with Burger Barn. Buy a stack, get a stack for free.

He had us all working day and night to meet some kind of pan-cake quota," Jilly replied.

We sat glumly. It would be pure torture playing softball with Mr. Cooper as a coach. And there was no sign of Jake.

"We've been had. I'm out of here."

"Jilly, this was your idea. We can't leave."

"Why not?"

I was about to respond, when Jake's car pulled up. My head swiveled like it was attached to a magnet. My eyes traced the way his shoulders made a perfect vee to his waist.

I shot a pleading look Jilly's way. "Please, please, please."

Just then Susi strutted by on her way to the bathroom.

"Hey, get a load of Mr. Cooper! I think he's checking out Susi Fielding." Something new had caught her attention. I was safe.

"Gross!" I studied Mr. Cooper. His tongue was practically hanging out. He was scouting something and it sure wasn't baseball talent. I swear I saw Susi fluttering her eyelashes at him.

Jilly just chuckled. "Blackmail material."

Jake came over and sat next to me, just as Mr. Cooper barked out an order. "Sinclair, you're up."

Great. I dragged my way up to bat.

After my second strike, Mr. Cooper was beet red and looked like he was going to explode. I waited patiently at the plate while he mumbled some utter crap about girls and sports. I was ready to show him how girls played, and pictured a softball hit right to Mr. Cooper's personal strike zone.

"Megan, I think you need a little one-on-one time with me. Coaching, that is." Mr. Cooper's face shone oily in the sun.

I choked on pure disgust. Was he insinuating what I thought he was?

"Hey, Mr. C., we're all a little rusty. How about if I work with Megan a little on her swing?" Jake to the rescue.

Mr. Cooper nodded once as he wiped his face with a handkerchief. His face returned to its normal pasty color.

My face, on the other hand, took on a rosy glow. I smiled to myself. Jake was sticking up for me.

We walked to a corner of the field to practice, so Jake could show me the right way to swing. I watched his shoulders and thought of all the things I'd like to practice with Jake. Softball was not at the top of my list.

I tried to concentrate as Jake helped me with my swing.

"Now you try, Megan." He reached over and with a gentle nudge, corrected my stance. For a minute there, I thought he was going to put his arms around me. To show me how to swing the bat, of course, just like in those corny movies.

The thought flashed through my mind that maybe I should play dumb, and then Jake would really put his arms around me. Nah. Not in front of the Pancake Palace crew. Besides, I wasn't very good at playing dumb.

After practice, a bunch of us hung around talking. Jake stood close to me, so close I could smell his fresh clean sweat. Jilly stopped dazzling Moldy Dave long enough to shoot me an I-know-what-you're-thinking stare. I crossed my eyes at her when I thought no one was watching, but Jake caught me and grinned.

All too soon, Jake dragged Moldy Dave away from Jilly. Jake's good-bye was for the group, but his smile was just for me. I stared dreamily after him, until I felt a sharp jab from Jilly's elbow.

I let the waves of idle chatter wash over me. Jake had smiled at me and all was right with the world.

But then, I caught a glimpse of Peter Fenton leaning against the fence. A gym bag and a bat were at his feet. I shivered. Despite the evidence of my own eyes, I wondered what he was doing there.

I knew he was staring at me. He was probably waiting for his team, I told myself, but suddenly I couldn't move. It was like he'd pinned me to the wall again, only this time with his eyes. I was relieved when some girl from school, a freshman, I think, rushed up to him. But she had to tug on his arm before he broke eye contact. My stomach twisted and I wanted to leave, to get away.

I rubbed my arms, trying to erase sudden goose bumps.

His teammates showed up, and Peter lost all interest in me. I noticed Brent Swenson, too. I dragged Jilly away from her recreational flirting and we walked to our cars. I decided it was an opportune time to make my getaway, before her matchmaking instinct kicked in.

Mrs. Westland, a week later, I was at work, kicking myself over the energy I'd wasted thinking about Jake. I convinced myself that Jake had no interest in me, and I had reason to believe it. After all, I hadn't even seen him in the last few days.

Jilly and I filled syrup containers to pass the time. It was quiet, late on a Saturday morning. The coffee drinkers had already staked out their territory at the counter and the Kiwanis were halfway into their meeting in the "Boremore Room," which is what we called the Balmoral Room. So I had plenty of time to brood.

Jake Darrow is a losing proposition. At least that's what I told myself over and over. I hadn't talked to him since softball practice, even though he was at work, too.

I don't know what I was expecting. He had a girlfriend, so it wasn't like he could just call me up and ask me out or anything. Even if he wanted to, that is. Besides, I'd be disappointed if he turned out to be like Sam or some of the other guys I knew.

What did I know about Jake Darrow, really? Just surface stuff. I imagined myself half in love with him and I didn't know one personal thing about him. I told myself to quit dreaming about Jake and get back to work. Taking my own advice, I headed to the back. The pie case needed to be stocked before the lunch rush.

Mr. Cooper stood in the back room, staring at Susi's ass as she tossed sourdough loaves into the bread warmer. Susi seemed oblivious to Mr. Cooper's creepiness. She gave him a smile as she headed for the front.

I grabbed a couple of apple pies and tried to beat a hasty exit.

Mr. Cooper's voice stopped me. "You're looking particularly lovely today, Megan."

"Thanks," I said. I meant *creep*.

I held up the pies and tried to pass, but Mr. Cooper took a step closer, brushing up against my breasts as he did. I stepped back.

"Excuse me," he said. *Yeah, right. What a perv.*

I practically ran to the front. My hands were shaking a little as I put the pies in the case. No way was I going back there again. That man was one big ball of ick.

I distracted myself by thinking about the plans for the evening. There was a big party at the Pit that night. The Pit is what we call the mined-out gravel pit a few miles from town. I hoped Jake would be there. It was supposed to be the event of the summer, with a barbecue, beer, and live music. Not to mention all the opportunities for more intimate socializing. Don't get me wrong, I wasn't thinking about anything more than talking to Jake.

Even if he broke up with Savannah, he had practically admitted he was interested in someone else. But I had to admit I was curious about why he'd pick me to tell who he was lusting after.

I almost choked on my gum when I realized I hoped he was lusting after me. I'd always admired Jake from afar, kind of like a kick-ass pair of designer jeans that you knew you'd look good in but was totally out of your price range.

The possibility of actually hooking up with Jake had never occurred to me before now. The thought of allowing just any guy's hands to roam all over my body was repugnant. But for some reason, the thought of Jake's hands touching me made my heart beat faster.

"Brent will be at the party tonight," Jilly said, snapping me out of my Jake-induced reverie.

"So?" I replied.

The party would rage on till morning or till we got caught, whichever came first. Usually after a few hours, the town cops came by any underage events, confiscated the alcohol, and drove the obviously wasted home to their loving parents.

"He's been asking you out for over a month. Doesn't he get points for trying?" Jilly was always trying to set me up with someone, but lately she'd really brought out the big guns. Brent Swenson was quarterback, honor society, and all-around nice guy. He made me want to yawn every time I saw him.

I stared at the cook's window. I could see Jake's back as he flipped pancakes. Jilly followed my gaze.

"Megan, I didn't want to say anything, but Butterball told me the other day that Savannah expects a promise ring when she gets back from Arizona."

Yikes. A promise ring. That was serious.

"And they've being going out for years," Jilly continued.

"Okay, I get it. Point made. If Brent asks me out, I'll go."

"Megan, I'm sorry. I just don't want to see you get hurt."

I hadn't told Jilly about my conversation with Jake. I don't know why. I guess maybe secretly I was hoping I was the girl he was tempted by. I didn't want anyone, not even my best friend, to burst that particular bubble.

A bus pulled up and a load of famished people streamed out. That was the last time Jilly and I had time to say much besides "hell" and "I need fifteen cinnamon rolls" and "two orders of bran cereal" until after lunch. The diner stayed busy during the summer with hordes of tourists passing through on their way to Minneapolis or Chicago. They never stayed in Fairview because there wasn't anything to see.

As usual, I was off before Jilly. So much for my college-tuition-slash-boob-job fund. I appraised my figure in the mirror by the time clock, and sighed. I punched out, counted my measly tips, and went in the back to change. I thought about sitting down for a soda before I left, but decided that was way too obvious.

I went into the bathroom to get out of my uniform. I changed into a pair of jean cutoffs and a sleeveless shirt and slipped some sandals on my feet. After running a brush through my hair and applying a little lip-gloss and lotion, I was ready.

Since the Beast was running well enough to risk the five-mile drive to the party, I had volunteered to pick up our contribution to the cookout/kegger. We had been assigned hot dog buns and shot glasses, a bizarre, but apparently necessary, combination.

I went out the back door as Mr. Cooper came in. He blocked my way.

As I said hi to him, I felt my bra strap slide down my shoulder. *Great, free peep show for the perv.*

I tried to shrug it back into place, but he was riveted to the sight of my thrashed old Maidenform.

His hand reached out and his finger tugged on the strap of my bra. I stood paralyzed, unable to believe he'd actually touched my bra, touched me. My stomach felt like I'd chugged a bottle of spoiled milk.

"Megan, please make sure you wear clean underthings when you come to work. I can help you with any hygiene issues you may have," he said. His eyes gleamed as he took a step closer. I took a step back and, without another word, he walked into his office and shut the door.

I couldn't move. My mouth was frozen open. My first reaction was to tell him my bra was not dirty, it was just old and beige. How dumb was that? Why did I feel like I had to justify the state of my underwear to my boss? As my brain processed what had happened, rage rampaged through my veins. What in the hell was going on? Was it me? What was so different about me that a grown man, my boss even, felt free to paw me? Two things immediately came to mind. My breast-reduction plan was becoming more and more appealing.

I slammed the back door as I left, hoping the bastard could hear it through his office door.

I leaned against the window of the Beast, taking in gulps of air. I felt like kicking something or someone.

Instead, I cranked my radio and took off in search of party supplies. When I arrived at the Pit, I parked my car near Jilly's. I saw her standing under a tree, talking to a bunch of guys from our school. Even though Jilly was extremely unavailable and let everyone know it, she was a man magnet. She saw me and cut through the crowd of her adoring fans to meet me. She handed me a small package.

"From Dad and Gold-Digger, I mean Stephanie. Their Paris trip. Open it. Open it." Jilly practically jumped up and down.

"They're back?" Jilly's parents were usually home about one week in four.

"Yep. For a few days. Next week Dad has to go to Austin to buy pigs or something."

I took the package. It was beautifully wrapped in some expensive grayish purple print with tiny orchids stamped over it. I carefully took the tape away from one corner and handed the wrapping to Jilly. I shook the box, but it didn't rattle. Probably clothes.

"Oh, you're taking forever. Let's see what you got!" She jumped up and down.

I held an itty-bitty piece of sea-foam green material in my hand.

"What is it?" I said, my stomach sinking. Jilly's stepmom had slutty taste.

"It's a swimsuit and it's a great color for you. Stephanie and Dad got me one, too."

"Mine's in a different size, I hope?"

"Yeah, Stephanie got you one size smaller—on top."

I was horrified, until I saw the wide grin on her face. "Very funny, Jilly. I don't think I'm ready to wear that, that, piece of tissue paper, even in the privacy of my own backyard."

An hour and two beers later, I had convinced myself it was a great idea. It just goes to show you how alcohol can make the stupidest idea seem reasonable. You try cramming major cleavage into bitty little triangles of material.

We went to the Porta Potti and Jilly guarded the door while I held my nose and changed.

The material was stretchy and it covered more than I thought it would, but not much more. I pulled my shorts back on and bravely exited the Porta Potti wearing the most indecent bikini top this small town had ever seen.

Jilly waited for me outside. She had taken off the shirt she wore over her swimsuit. Her suit was the same style as mine, only in blue. She didn't look nearly as obscene as I felt.

She grabbed my arm, and handed me back my beer, and whispered, "Megan, if it makes you uncomfortable, save the bikini for your backyard."

"I'll wear it." It was the liquid courage talking.

"Brent is here and he asked me where you were," she whispered.

Before I could answer her, another car roared up. Jake hopped out and walked over to where we stood.

"Hi, Jilly, hi, Megan." Oh, great. Just what I need: the guy I have a crush on and the guy who has a crush on me, both at the same party. Jake wore a blue shirt and khaki shorts. Did I say *yum* before?

Jake Darrow was looking good. And I definitely was doing some looking. It seemed as though Jake was doing some looking, too. Miracle of miracles, it was into my eyes. Not the first place a guy usually looks—well, at me, anyway.

"Want to go for a swim?" Behind his back, Jilly shook her

head. I replied before my brain could tell my heart what a dumb idea it was.

"Sure," I replied. "Let me grab a towel."

"Hey, wait up, Megan. I'll come, too." Jilly tagged at our heels.

Moldy Dave was already staked out by the keg. Probably waiting for someone to splat something interesting onto the ground. Jake stopped to fill up a glass, while I went to the car to get my towel. Jilly trailed me while I pulled out lotion and the Hello Kitty towel she'd given me for my fourteenth birthday.

As we got to my car, Brent wandered by. Jilly elbowed me in the ribs.

"Jilly, please cut it out. Stop trying so hard to set me up with someone. I'm perfectly happy being single."

"Megan, you know Brent's crazy about you. Can't you just give him a chance?"

"I said I'd go out with him if he asked again, and I will. But that doesn't mean I have to spend every waking minute with him."

I stomped back to where Brent and Jake stood talking. Jilly followed close behind.

We joined a game of water volleyball as they were choosing up sides. Somehow Brent and Jilly ended up on one side and Jake and I were on the other. He stood in front of me to my left, where I could get a good view of his tanned shoulders.

We played several games. I'm normally halfway decent at volleyball. It's one of the few sports I don't totally detest. Don't ask me why or how, but I have a mean serve.

I was having a great time, till that sleaze Peter Fenton showed up.

Chapter

5

Mrs. Westland, I'll bet you remember Peter. He's hard to forget—and I mean that in the worst possible way.

It was obvious that Peter Fenton had started his own private party several hours ago. He stood at the water's edge, swaying like a sailor in a high wind. He was using Butterball as his personal ballast.

I wondered briefly what had happened to last minute's girl, the freshman. Got a life and a clue, probably. I can't believe girls find Peter remotely appealing. But Butterball obviously did. I wondered if she had any idea what he was really like.

Peter and Butterball watched us play.

Butterball shot me a he's-my-man stare and then, to advertise her new ownership, turned and snuggled into Peter's side. She whispered something in his ear and cuddled closer.

She was welcome to him. I almost felt sorry for her. I tried to get back into the game, but I felt Peter's bleary-eyed attention ooze all the way down my body.

Now half my serves were hitting the net. My coordination was all off. Jake shot me an encouraging smile, but I couldn't get back into the game.

Uneasy, I glanced over at them again. Peter's beady eyes drifted over my body and stopped dead center at my chest. I swear a little dribble of drool trailed down his chin.

It reminded me of when he had pinned me up against the wall, with his hands all over me. Something I really didn't want to remember.

I couldn't really see letting anyone touch me there, but the thought of Peter's hands on my breasts made me ill. My swimsuit became unbearably tiny. A shiver went up my spine and I noticed that the sky had turned a funny gray color.

I went over to Jilly. "I'm going to the car to get my shirt. I'm a little cold."

"And Peter Fenton's feeling a little hot," she observed. "Want me to come with?"

Peter seemed totally engrossed in chugging as much beer as humanly possible, with Butterball stapled to his side. Two potential problems out of the way.

"Nah, I'll be okay. Send out the search party if I'm not back in ten minutes." I shivered again as I left the water. I stopped to grab my towel and headed for my car.

I almost made it, but Peter slithered quietly like the snake he is. I didn't see him until the last minute.

"Hi, Megan," he said. He smiled a crocodile smile. Nausea rumbled in my stomach. "You're lookin' good."

My power of speech disappeared. I watched him. He continued to smile as he moved closer. "Wanna do something next weekend?"

My mind flashed to Peter Fenton's definition of "doing something."

I managed to spit out a "no thanks." I tried to keep it neutral, but I think it came out with a not-in-this-life tone.

He stepped closer. "I've had my eye on you. And what Peter Fenton wants, he gets."

My mind reeled at his threat.

"I try not to date people who refer to themselves in the third person." My smart-ass line sounded weak and uncertain, even to my own ears.

I tried a strategic retreat. He blocked my way.

Peter grabbed my wrist and wouldn't let go. "Megan, you bitch! You think you and your tits are so special."

A drunken dumb jock harassing a girl always attracts a scene, and this was no exception. As Peter's ugly taunts about my breasts got louder, the crowd grew. But nobody did anything.

I kind of tuned him out for a minute or two. I silently stood there as garbage spewed out of his mouth. The things he said were low, even for Peter. I didn't want to give him the satisfaction of knowing he'd hurt me.

I cut Peter off in mid-tirade. "Peter, my boob vocabulary is well developed. I can even recite the list alphabetically, want to hear? Bongos, boobs, cantaloupes, chi-chis, grapefruits, headlights, high beams, Himalayas, honkers, hooters, jugs, marangas, melons, mountains, ta-tas, taters, tits, tomatoes, watermelons, and yams."

Hot tears drifted down my face, one by one, but I ignored them. Peter stood there, a stupid smirk on his face.

"I turned you down and now you're pissed, not to mention drunk. There are plenty of other stupid girls out there who will put up with your shit. I won't. Just leave me alone, Peter." I stepped closer and tapped him on the shoulder for emphasis.

He went down like a load of bricks. I thought that somehow I'd hurt him, but when I bent down to check on him, he'd only passed out.

The crowd cheered and clapped. It's frightening how easily the mob turns. I faced them. "Now, will someone drive this idiot home before he kills himself? I've had all the fun I can take." And I marched to my car.

"Megan, wait up." It was Jake. Oh, great, he must have seen the whole thing. I sat on the hood of my car and waited while he caught up to me. I kept my head down, hoping he wouldn't see me crying.

When Jake reached my car, he put his hand on my shoulder. Not in a creepy Peter Fenton, I-want-your-bod kind of way.

"Hey, are you okay?" Jake said, and gently brushed the hair away from my face. I couldn't believe how sweet he was. "Are you cold? Want me to drive you home?"

"No, I'm fine. I just want to get out of here."

"I didn't see what happened. Was Peter bothering you?"

I couldn't speak, so I just nodded.

"You're a good person. He's an idiot. How about if I follow you just to make sure you make it home all right?" I couldn't see his face. He seemed to be talking to his toes.

"Jake, I don't know if that's such a good idea—you know how everyone gossips."

"Don't worry about it, Megan, I'll just follow you. I won't even get out of my car, I promise."

I drove home with Jake following in his car. When we reached my driveway, Jake waited as I pulled in.

I stopped by his window. "Thanks, Jake. I really appreciate it."

"Megan, I know it's not the time right now, but I'd like to talk to you soon, okay?"

"Okay, Jake. Thanks again."

He watched, with the motor running, as I unlocked the door and went inside. A horn sounded a good-bye, and I heard his car roar off.

I stood inside the door and watched him leave, thinking it was a good thing we'd been in separate cars. Jake was so sweet. Dangerously sweet.

Messing around with someone who had a girlfriend was only asking for trouble. So why did the thought refuse to leave my head? It took me a long time to get to sleep that night.

Wrestling with your conscience does tend to cut into getting some z's.

Chapter

6

Mrs. Westland, Jake and I were working every shift together, but we never seemed to find time for that talk. Susi Fielding was scheduled for most of the crappy closing shifts. I could look forward to work, without Mr. Cooper breathing down my neck—plus Jake on every shift.

Mr. Cooper said he switched to the night shift so he could go to church with his wife and kids on Sundays. The assistant manager, Joan Stevens, who also did double duty as a hostess, was a married mom with older kids. She loved working days so she could spend evenings with her family. Mr. Cooper was in a better mood and he hadn't given me any oily compliments. He even let Jilly leave early sometimes.

It was Saturday. Jake, Jilly, and I were all working the morning shift. I knew Jilly suspected there was something going on between Jake and me. I suspected it, too. I just wasn't sure what it was.

There was always a lull between breakfast and lunch, which

is when one of the waitresses had to set up the salad bar. It was my turn, so I headed to the back kitchen.

Jilly told me that salad bar prep used to be the cook's job, until someone put something too gross to mention in one of the salad dressings. The rumor must have gotten out, because most people won't touch our salads, not even the vegetarians.

I pulled a stack of stainless steel containers out of the rack and went into the walk-in fridge to get the potato salad and the other assorted high-caloric delicacies making up our salad bar. After plopping heaping ladles of gooey stuff into the containers, I set them on the cart and reached for the dressing ladles. They hung on a hook just beyond my reach. As I stretched up to get them, someone pressed up against my back.

"Let me help you," Jake said in my ear. He put an arm around my waist with one hand and reached up and grabbed the ladles.

I could feel his warmth, through our clothes, all the way to my skin. All I could think was *Oh, my god. I probably have b.o. It's busy on Saturdays and I always sweat buckets.*

One of Jake's arms remained around me as he set the ladles down. He bent in and nuzzled my neck. My whole body buzzed like it had been plugged into a light socket.

"Mmm, you smell good," he said, "like maple syrup." He brushed his lips across the expanse of my bare neck. I'd never noticed how vulnerable my neck was. Mr. Cooper made us scrape every strand of hair up into a tight bun and stuff it under our caps. It had never seemed sexy before now.

Jilly must have some sort of chastity radar, because right then, she ran into the back. "Megan, it's almost time for the lunch rush. Did the closers forget to restock the salad bar again?"

Jake released me and strolled through the open doorway into the grill area. He was whistling. I still stood rooted to the spot, staring at the salad bar in utter stupefaction. Jilly's worried look screamed, *He's got a girlfriend!*

The rest of my shift flew by. After work, Jilly and I decided to stay and eat lunch. We had the afternoon-shift waitress write up our ticket, and took it to the till to get our discounted price. Jilly paid half price, too, even though her dad owned the place.

Jake popped around from the back kitchen. He set our burgers down at the break table and snagged a fry off my plate.

"What're you guys doing after work?"

"This is it," Jilly replied for both of us.

"Want to practice?"

"Practice what?" I said rapidly. Jilly gave me a disgusted look that said, *Get your mind out of the gutter, Sinclair.*

Jake laughed, like I'd said something witty. "Softball, of course." He paused and met my eyes. "Unless you have something better in mind."

Jilly almost choked on a French fry. Later, when Jake went

into the walk-in fridge, I said, low and light, "It'll be fun, Jilly, please."

"Some fun," she replied. "What does Jake Darrow have in mind for you, Megan? He's been looking at you like you're the syrup on his short stack. Besides, the slumber party is tonight."

"That doesn't start until seven."

Mrs. Westland, I had to resort to friendship blackmail to get my way. A little reminder of eighth grade, when I covered for Jilly to sneak out and meet Tommy Gerenson. We told Jake we'd meet him at the park at three, when he got off.

Jilly and I went to my house to change. I couldn't believe it. I got all jittery. What was happening? Jake Darrow possibly, maybe, liked me! I ignored the part of my brain that jeered, *remember what happened with Sam—you thought he liked you for you, too. But we know what he was really after.*

But at practice, Jake was all business and softball. He ran us ragged, practicing my swing and Jilly's catch.

By the time I made it home, I barely had time to shower and get ready for the slumber party. I ached all over, but I couldn't miss the slumber party. It was tradition.

"Megan, are you home?" It was my mom.

"Hi, Mom. I'm in here."

When my mom came into my room, she was positively haggard.

"It seems like I haven't seen you all summer," she said, and put her hand on my hair. "The twins are going through the terrible twos."

"Which set?" I joked.

We shared a smile.

"What's your schedule like? I wanted to go school clothes shopping. Just the two of us. We could drive up to Minneapolis and spend the night."

"That'd be great, Mom. My chemistry final is in a couple of weeks. How about after that?"

"Sounds good." There was a comfortable silence.

"Where are you off to tonight?" Most people hate when their parents ask where they're going. But it had been so long since Mom had had any time for me, I felt a warm glow.

"Annual slumber party. Dad said it was okay," I said, jangling my car keys.

"Be careful," Mom called after me.

I pulled up to Jilly's house, avoiding the temptation to drive just a few doors down to see if Jake was home.

We've had the slumber party every year since we were in junior high. Summer wasn't summer until we all went swimming at the Pit at midnight. Every year it was at a different house, but every year we did the same thing: Tell ghost stories, swim, stay up late eating and drinking and talking about everyone we know.

In junior high, it was just soda and chips. We'd graduated

to beer sophomore year. This year, Jilly broke out a bottle of Southern Comfort from her dad's bar.

There were ten of us. We all used to be super close, but we'd kind of broken up into little cliques since junior high, although in a town the size of Fairview, everyone hung out with everyone at least some of the time. The town was too small for real cliques.

Everyone was in Jilly's bedroom. I sat down across from Amanda Marcus. She represented the loner, stoner crowd. Then there was Tessa Jude. She represented the party-girl crowd.

Jilly represented the popular people. Even though Jilly was one of the most popular people in school, she didn't act like it. I guess I must represent the brains. Or the boobs.

Everyone talked at once. Talking was always first on the agenda. Jilly handed me a drink when I got there.

"'My advice to you is to start drinking heavily,'" I quoted as I took the drink.

"That's an easy one. *Animal House*. 1978."

How did she do it? I could never stump Jilly, but I liked to try.

I sat back and smiled. I took a sip of my Southern and Seven.

"You're going to need an artificial stimulant," she said, "since Butterball's here."

Great. I guess Butterball Belling was there to represent the coy, backstabbing wannabes. Butterball's the worst gossip in town. Worse than the old men who sit on benches and watch everything that happens. Which isn't much. Mostly, they report any kids getting out of hand to their parents. Butterball was much worse. She was totally malicious, but she still got invited every year. Old habit, I guess.

I was laughing with Susi and Jilly about the time we almost got caught toilet-papering Ryan Donahue's house, when I heard Jake's name. I wasn't expecting his name to be brought up tonight. I must have seemed a little more interested than was normal, because Jilly shot me a quick warning look. Butterball would love to find out I had a crush on Jake. And she was a friend of Jake's girlfriend, Savannah. At least, as much of a friend as Butterball could be.

"Anyway, Savannah said that she told Jake she needed some space so . . ."

I couldn't hear the rest of what Butterball said, but my heart gave this huge jump. I felt like everyone in the room could hear it pounding. I sat too far away to hear the rest because for once, Butterball talked in a low voice. Jilly was closer, and I saw her lean in a little, trying to do so inconspicuously.

"Oh, of course, they'll still get married. Don't be silly. Savannah wants to play before . . ."

Damn. Butterball's shrill voice faded in and out.

My mind raced. Could this be why Jake had been so flirtatious lately? It hadn't seemed like him to flirt with me behind his girlfriend's back. Was he just lonely because he'd been dumped?

I wanted to avoid Butterball's eye, so I wandered over to the stereo. I shuffled through the music selection, trying to find something festive. Jilly had a huge music collection. Butterball joined me. "So, Megan, I hear you and Peter had a bad fight at the Pit the other night."

Great. Butterball wanted to rehash yesterday's moldy news. I could feel it coming. She wanted to give me a hard time about Peter. She's had a crush on him since sixth grade.

She was going out with him and she wanted to rub it in. Like I cared. She was welcome to that skanky jock on a rope. I wondered if Pete's handsome face fooled her. Or if she even cared what was inside the pretty package. I decided to take the offensive.

"He asked me out and I said no. Why, are you interested? I can give you his number." Take that.

"No, thanks, I already have it. I'm not worried about competition from you. Peter can't wait to see me. In fact—" She broke off, giggling like a madwoman.

"Butterball, what's up?" Oops. That was a mistake. She hated to be called by her nickname. Who could blame her? She flounced off.

"Laura, wait, what do you mean?" It was too late. She'd marched upstairs to one of the bathrooms and slammed the door.

I knew Butterball. She was such a horny wench she couldn't go one night without fawning all over some guy, any guy.

I went over to Jilly to warn her. "Something's up. I think Butterball expects company of the male persuasion tonight."

"Well, that's just great. Lyle's at a baseball tournament."

Someone started a game of quarters, so the Pit wasn't mentioned till several hours and shots later.

Michelle and Cindy, the two nondrinkers in our little group, drove us to the Pit. It was almost midnight. Jilly and I changed into swimsuits, but a couple of girls decided to go natural. We weren't planning to do much swimming. Even in our intoxicated state, we knew swimming and drinking don't really mix.

We piled out of the cars and Tessa Jude and Lisa Aldrich immediately stripped. They must have heard that some guys would be showing up when we got back, so they wanted to make it quick to get back to the real fun, which for them meant anything that included a penis.

"C'mon, Megan, let's go!" Jilly grabbed my hand and we ran into the water. It was freezing. Technically, we were trespassing, but Mr. Keller, the owner, never cared as long as we left it the way we found it. At least, that's what I heard. Nobody's ever actually met Mr. Keller.

Swimming in the dark was strange. It felt like we were the only people left in the world. The moon floated in the sky like a big glass bubble.

It was so quiet, except for the crickets chirping their

summer song. I thought I heard a car door slam, somewhere in the distance. "You guys, I think I heard something."

"You're imagining things, Megan. It must be all that reading you do." From Butterball, of course. I'm not sure she even knows *how* to read. She never lifts a book, just asks some guy to help her with her homework, even though she doesn't really need the help. Any guy will do, even a dumb one.

I turned and floated on my back, with the moon shining down on me. I thought how much I'd like to be with Jake on a night like this. I heard another car door slam. "You guys, I'm sure I heard something."

"Megan, I think I heard something, too." That from Jilly.

"I didn't hear a thing." Butterball again.

Lisa and Tessa were already out of the water, standing buck naked and shivering. "Let's go back, you guys. We're freezing."

"Okay, let's go."

I heard a high-pitched shriek from Butterball. Oh, my God! I dropped the flashlight. Footsteps crunched, fast as gunshots, through the underbrush.

What happened? My heart pounded. Jilly and I headed toward the sound. Then I heard a giggle and "Oh, Peter."

It sounded like Butterball couldn't wait. There were several more pseudo-shrieks, followed by giggles, as, one by one, the girls in our group paired off with their obviously preplanned surprise visitors. I couldn't see her, but I knew Jilly was shrugging and heading for her car.

I was on my way back. I hadn't found the flashlight. Besides, I didn't want to be anywhere near Peter Fenton, even if he was occupied with Butterball. From the sounds of the whispers and soft moans, it was time for me to leave or I'd be hearing more than my virginal ears bargained for.

I felt a hand on my arm and froze.

"Megan, it's me." I had to be dreaming. It sounded like Jake.

"Jake, is that you?" I whispered.

"Yes, it's me." Jake wrapped an arm around my shoulders and pulled me close.

"What are you doing here?"

"When Kevin told me about the raid, I figured you'd be here. Let's go."

"Where are we going?"

"You'll see." When I gazed into his eyes, I knew I'd follow him anywhere.

Chapter
7

Mrs. Westland, when we walked to Jake's car, a couple was making out, leaning against his car for leverage. It was Tessa Jude and Rob Enders. I couldn't even look at Jake. I was afraid he would be able to see the thoughts running through my head. I wondered what it would be like to kiss Jake. When the love-birds came up for air, I asked them about Jilly. I got a brief "went home," before lip-lock resumed.

I didn't want to go back to Jilly's, where I was pretty sure the duos by the lake would eventually show up. I mean, why not? Parents gone, huge house, multiple bedrooms. Jake smiled at me, and I pushed away the little thought that one of those bedrooms was reserved for me. I didn't have to worry about Jilly. She'd probably call Lyle, who gave Jilly something she'd never had before: undivided attention and love. He would have been waiting patiently for just such an opportunity.

Jake and I drove around for a little bit. He didn't seem to have anything urgent on his mind, although he acted like he wanted to say something a couple of times. Instead, he reached over and fiddled with his car stereo, asked me if I was cold, and generally fidgeted.

I was still stunned that Jake had wanted to find me and I kept turning it around in my mind.

Then I remembered two highly important facts: I was wearing nothing but a wet swimsuit and there was nobody home at my house. Dennis and David were on dates. Mom and Dad were over at Great-aunt Cecelia's playing bridge or something equally exciting. Of course, Mom couldn't bear to leave the little guys, so she took them with.

Mrs. Westland, don't let the "great-aunt" part fool you. Aunt Ce-Ce was seventy-five and still kept my parents out really late. I had the house to myself.

"Nobody's home at my house."

Jake immediately swung the car around and made a left toward my neighborhood. Hmm. Maybe he'd changed his mind about whatever he was going to say and was just planning on dropping me off at my house.

Nope. As I expected and feverishly hoped, Jake and I had the place to ourselves. We stood in the living room, not saying anything, until I remembered I was still wearing my suit. It was getting clammy.

"Uh, I'm going to go change."

"Okay." I watched him for a clue. Nothing.

I headed to my room, threw on some clothes, and raced back downstairs. First to the kitchen, where I grabbed two glasses of lemonade. Deep breathing exercises. I put my face against the slider glass. Being alone with Jake was hard on my central nervous system.

I peered outside as I took some calming breaths. The whole town seemed to be asleep. I couldn't hear anything except the sound of the wind in the trees. Everything was peaceful and still. Through the slider, I could see a silver moon. And Jake.

Jake in the moonlight. What a sight. He had wandered out back and was sitting in the hammock under our oak tree, so I took the lemonade outside. Maybe that would make him talk. Something was on his mind.

"Did you want to talk about something, Jake?" I set the lemonade down on a little table and sat next to him in the hammock.

"I broke up with Savannah because I've been thinking about you all the time." His words came out jumbled, like one big long word. I was still trying to comprehend what he was telling me, when he spoke again.

"Can I have some lemonade?"

He was nervous. I couldn't believe it. Jake Darrow was nervous.

"Sure. Help yourself." My mind was reeling. Jake Darrow liked me.

Jake reached over and grabbed an ice cube out of the glass. I saw it coming, but couldn't get out of the way in time. Ice cube down my back.

"Hey, cut it out!" I said. "Just you wait until I get my hands on you." I got out of the hammock to reach my glass of lemonade, but Jake grabbed it and dangled it out of reach.

I twisted and shifted my weight, laughing helplessly as Jake tickled me. We fell with a plop into the hammock. The hammock swayed and, for a minute, I thought it would tip us both out, but Jake steadied it with one hand.

Another application of cool ice on my skin made me realize Jake was really there, next to me. We lay there for a minute, out of breath from laughing. I was very aware of Jake's leg pressing against mine. Somehow, our hands entwined. He said my name softly and then he kissed me. A long, sweet kiss. He tasted like summer.

I kissed him back and adjusted my position to get closer. Just a little closer. His hands were smooth on my skin. He ran his leg up and down against mine. His lips trailed up and down my neck. His teeth grazed the skin on the nape of my neck, sending little shock waves all over my body.

We stayed in the hammock for a long time. I knew that someone would come home eventually. We needed to stop kissing, but we couldn't.

I'd never been kissed like that. Long, deep, worshipping kisses. I felt like I was dissolving, like we both would dissolve.

We'd melt together on the hammock and days later they'd find us. An unidentifiable lump of passion.

Distantly, I heard a car door slam. Jake hesitated, and then went back to kissing me. I didn't want to stop, either, but I thought of my mom's face if she came home to find me making out with one of Dennis and David's friends. She'd never leave me alone again. I nudged Jake and cut the last kiss short. Jake climbed out of the hammock just in time. He was tucking his shirt in when Dennis and David came charging through the slider.

"Hey, Jake, what are you doing here?" Dennis stared at me with an odd expression. I wondered what I looked like to him. Probably like I'd been making out for the last hour. Dennis always was sharper than David. Overprotective, too.

I straightened up and hoped there wasn't any stray lipstick on Jake's face, or anywhere else.

"You were supposed to meet us at Keith's, not here!" David chimed in. He grinned. "Sorry you had to hang around my baby sister. What did you guys do to kill the time?" he added innocently.

"Yeah, Jake, what did you do to pass the time?" Dennis added, with a glint in his eye. Uh-oh.

"We've been hanging out waiting for you guys to get back." I spoke quickly, hoping to deflect the questions I saw in Dennis's face.

I heard my parents' car pull up. Dennis met my eyes and I

could see that he knew exactly how I'd been entertaining his best friend. I hoped he wouldn't tell Mom.

I could only imagine what my mom would have said if she had caught Jake and me in the hammock. I think my dad would have been pretty cool about it, but my mom? She would have flipped. I jumped out of the hammock and headed for the kitchen. Jake and the twins followed me. No one said a word.

I heard my dad head upstairs to put Dakota and Dillon to bed. My mom walked into the kitchen a minute later.

Jake was not in the least embarrassed to almost get caught making out with his best friends' sister.

"Hello, Jake. Did you boys have a nice time tonight?" My mom sounded sweet as sugar when she talked to anybody besides me.

"Dennis and I just got home. Jake was already here," David blabbed, and he didn't even realize he was doing it.

As usual, my mother took the first opportunity to criticize me. "Megan, for heaven's sakes, why didn't you offer Jake any refreshment?"

"I think Jake got plenty, Mom. Lemonade, I mean." Dennis sounded like the model of innocence. I flipped him off when I thought Mom wasn't paying attention.

"Hey, guys, want to go get a burger or something?" Jake said.

Dennis relaxed then, but he raised his eyebrows to let me know I wasn't off the hook. "Sure, Jake, why not?"

Jake turned to me, and with a totally charming smile, said,

"Thanks for the lemonade, Megan. I'll see you tomorrow night at work."

Tomorrow night at work? Jake had my schedule confused. I wasn't on the schedule for the next two nights. As a matter of fact, neither was he. Jake watched me as the realization dawned on my face.

Unfortunately, my mother was watching, too. She stood there with her arms crossed and her head swiveling from Jake to me.

I replied, "Yeah, Jake, see you at six tomorrow."

My mom and I watched Jake and the twins leave, and then I said good night and made a hasty retreat. She didn't say anything at first, and I thought for once that she wasn't going to give me the third degree. Convinced I was off the hook, I went to bed and dreamed about Jake.

The next day, I was in my room, talking on the phone with Jilly.

"Jake Darrow and I made out. At my house, in the hammock," I said.

"You *what?!*" Jilly's scream hit an all-time high.

"Don't worry. He broke up with Savannah."

"I can't believe it. I thought he was just flirting while she was out of town." Surprise made Jilly blunt.

"He said he'd been thinking about me lately," I said, suddenly shy. I'd never had much to tell Jilly before, except how drunk Sam had been at the last beer blast.

We spent the next hour on the phone, trying to figure out what I'd wear to meet Jake. Finally, I hung up and told her I'd see her tomorrow.

My mom waited until then to give me the talk. Sometimes I wondered if my dad had been some huge sex fiend when they met or something. My mom was so worried about my sex life, imaginary though it was.

She tapped on my open door. Her eagle eyes scoped out my favorite outfits on the bed and she frowned.

"Megan, I wanted to talk to you about something."

"What, Mom?" Here it comes.

I grabbed my favorite jeans and a deep blue top and headed for my closet, hoping she'd get the hint. She didn't. I took off my T-shirt and threw it in the hamper and quickly pulled the blue top over my head, hoping my mother would just go away.

Instead, she stuck her head inside the closet as I was wiggling into my jeans. "Megan, this is important."

"What did I do wrong this time, Mom?"

"What makes you think you did anything wrong? Did you?" My mom's voice was calm, but I could sense the tension in the stiff way she stood.

"No, Mom, I didn't do anything wrong. But it seems like the only time we have a conversation is when you think I've done something."

"It's just . . ." She paused. "I saw the way Jake was looking at you."

As irritated as I was, the thought that Jake was looking at me gave me a little thrill.

"You need to be careful."

"Careful of what? Jake hasn't even asked me out and you already have him seducing me." I tried to block out the night before from my mind.

"Boys Jake's age have only one thing on their minds."

"Dennis and David are Jake's age, but you don't give them a lecture every time they look at a girl." I turned away from her. My own mother didn't trust me.

"Megan, that's not the point. The point is that girls like you have to be extra careful."

I gulped away the tears. Girls like me? What did that mean?

"Thanks for the vote of confidence, Mom. I've got to go." I slid shoes on my feet and headed for the door.

"Where are you going?" My mother rarely raised her voice, but her volume control was on loud as she followed me into the hallway.

"Where *girls like me* usually go, Mom. To meet a guy." Then I swept past my astonished mother and got in the Beast and drove away.

Chapter 8

Mrs. Westland, have you ever liked someone so much
that when you're with him it seems like a dream?
That's how I felt. Jake was nowhere to be seen.
Maybe I'd just dreamed the whole incredible thing.

As I pulled into the parking lot of the Pancake Palace, I
wondered what I was doing there. If Jake really was interested in me, then why were we sneaking around, if that's even
what we were doing? Maybe he wanted to be able to blow me
off without my two big brothers around?

The parking lot was crowded, so I pulled around the rear of
the restaurant to park. Mr. Cooper told me he preferred to
have "that monstrosity you drive" parked there. I saw Susi's
car and a few others I recognized.

I sat in my car for a minute, trying to figure out where exactly I was supposed to meet Jake. Or if I even wanted to. I
noticed Susi was in her car with someone. I gave a little wave,
but she acted like she didn't see me. She started her car and
pulled away. The passenger seemed a little familiar. Maybe her
dad was in town.

Jake's car was parked in the corner, near a lamppost. I got out of my car and sat on the curb. I couldn't see for sure if he was in the car, but figured he must be. Well, he could come and get me if he wanted to talk to me. I sat twiddling my thumbs for about fifteen minutes. It seemed like we had a standoff.

Susi came back about fifteen minutes later and pulled around to the back door. I craned my neck to see if there was anyone else in the car, but the Dumpster blocked my view. Maybe she had bank deposit duty tonight.

I was walking back to my car when Butterball's car pulled up. Oh, great.

"Hi, Megan. What ya doin'?" I reluctantly went up to the driver's side. Butterball's friend Stacy Malloy was in the passenger seat.

"Hi, Laura, hi, Stacy." Butterball was everywhere this summer. You might think that because Laura's nickname was "Butterball" she was fat. Nope. She wasn't fat. You may not have noticed, but she has an unusual shape. Ever see a turkey? Small head, skinny arms and legs, and a big back end? That was Butterball.

"Who're you waiting for? We saw you sitting on the curb." Jesus, Butterball could collect more trash than Fairview Sanitation. Just what I needed. Great.

"I was waiting for my work schedule. The manager posts it Sunday night." It was true.

"Isn't that Jake Darrow's car over there?" I felt uncomfortable under her bug-eyed stare.

"He works here, too. Maybe he's working tonight, I don't know." I tuned out while Butterball droned on about the boring night she'd had so far.

I'd better go check the schedule, anyway. Now that school was out, Mr. Cooper was scheduling me for lots of early shifts.

I cut her off in mid-gossip. "I've got to go. See you around." I didn't know where Jake was. Maybe he really was working.

I walked through the front doors just as a huge crowd of people pushed through. I recognized a bunch of kids from the high school the next town over. Besides Ames, we had the only movie theater for miles, even if it was only open three nights a week.

I didn't see Jake. Where was he? I went to the back. Near the manager's office was a bulletin board with the schedule written in ink, near the time clock. I wrote down my schedule. Friday night, Saturday morning, Sunday morning.

Great, there was supposed to be a party Friday night, and Jilly and I both had to work the early bird shift on Saturday. I was, no surprise, first off on Friday night. I let my eyes casually wander over to Jake's schedule. He was working the same shifts as me, plus a Wednesday-morning shift.

An envelope for me was pinned to the bulletin board. I didn't recognize the bold handwriting, but put it in my pocket. I thought it was a tip package. If we left before a table did, the waitress still on duty was honor-bound to put the tip in a tiny envelope and tack it to the schedule board. I'd turned my only open table over to Susi, who wasn't exactly known for making sure tips went to the rightful owner.

Still no Jake.

Mr. Cooper walked by, crowding close as I stood in the hall. "Hi, Megan. What are you up to?"

I didn't like the way he said it or how he ogled me. I stared at him, hoping that some of my disgust registered.

"Checking the schedule?" he added in a normal tone.

"Yeah, hi, Mr. Cooper. Is that a new tie?" I took a step back and pretended to examine his tie. Anything to put a few feet between us.

He preened, obviously assuming I agreed with his fashion choice of red and purple angels. "It matches the restaurant's decor." Well, that was certainly nothing to brag about.

I wanted to say something snide, but really, Mr. Cooper, despite his innuendos, wasn't responsible for my bad mood. Jake Darrow was. Where the hell was he?

I sat at the counter. I hadn't had dinner. Moldy Dave waved from the kitchen window. Needless to say I just ordered a soda. After about five minutes of staring at the counter, the place I'd been working my butt off at not more than twenty-four hours ago, I decided to leave.

As I got up, I remembered the tip packet. I opened it, but it wasn't money. It was a tiny folded-up note.

Meet me in the Balmoral Room.
Jake

Oh, great. I'd been sitting around waiting for him outside for the last half hour and he'd been inside playing secret agent man. I had to wonder how he managed to get seated in that section, which was reserved for Kiwanis meetings and other large parties.

The lights were usually off in the Balmoral Room and the partition pulled closed. I walked to the rear of the restaurant. This was also the section without any windows. I guess Jake didn't want to be seen with me.

The practical part of my brain screamed, *He just broke up with his girlfriend, idiot.* But the vain part was miffed.

The partition was ajar and I could see the flicker of a candle. I wanted to reach for the light, but thought better of it. Maybe it was a practical joke.

Jake sat at a booth in the back. Candlelight framed his face. He was pissed.

"Hi."

"Hi." That was short.

Yikes. He was worse than Jilly when he was mad. I'd better say something before he exploded. "I was—er, waiting for you outside."

He relaxed. "Oh. I thought we should talk."

Obviously, Jake was not used to waiting. I guess Savannah's

a punctual little thing. It was not the best strategy to be thinking about the girlfriend of the guy you'd been in a hammock
with the night before. Ex-girlfriend, I corrected myself. My
brain was still having a hard time getting around the fact that
Jake had broken up with Savannah.

Uh-oh, here it comes. It was the "I like you a lot, Megan,
but Savannah and I are meant to be" talk. I'd read it in every
the-other-woman saga published. Or maybe I'd get the she-
just-doesn't-understand-me line.

That line seems to have worked well for Jilly's dad. He
ended up with a new wife not more than ten years older than
his daughter. I knew it. Why did I get involved with someone
who's already involved?

Jake's lips were moving, but my mind was rushing through
every sad story I'd heard. His words were like a white sheet of
noise. Finally, my mind stopped swirling and I focused on what
he was saying. "I know I told you Savannah and I decided to
take a break and see other people. I've been wanting to ask you
out for a long . . ."

He trailed off. "Are you okay, Megan? You seem a little
spaced out."

Spaced out? I'd been waiting for this moment since eighth
grade. And he wondered why I was a little spacey.

"Are you hungry? We could get something to eat?"

"No, let's just get out of here, okay?" We walked outside. I
didn't feel like I had to be skulking anymore. We even used the

front door and Jake took my hand as we strolled out. Butterball was already gone. She'd missed the scoop of the summer.

We left my car at the Palace and drove around in Jake's car, then stopped at the park. There was only one streetlight on, so most of the park was pitch-black, but we went for a walk anyway. Or maybe that was the idea. I wanted to ask him more about Savannah, but didn't want to ruin the moment.

"You're quiet," Jake said.

"So are you."

Just then every sprinkler in the park went on, soaking us to the skin. But I didn't care because I was in Jake's arms and he was kissing me.

Unfortunately, the fight with my mother lingered in my mind. I couldn't get her words out of my head.

"Jake, no." I pulled away. "Let's go." I walked back toward the car.

"Megan, wait a minute. What's the matter?"

I stood under the streetlight, feeling safer in the light. I knew Jake wouldn't do anything I didn't want to do. I wasn't afraid of him, I was afraid of myself.

"We're just going so fast. Last month, you were dating Savannah and you were the perfect couple."

"And you dated Sam. So what? He's in the past, just like Savannah."

"I just don't know, Jake. Let's just slow down a little, okay?"

The light threw shadows on Jake's face. It made him look

closed, unapproachable, and definitely pissed off. "Megan, it's simple. You either want to go out with me or you don't."

To make matters worse, Butterball's Honda cruised by as we stood there. She was gawking so hard she almost hit the curb. I knew it would be all over town tomorrow.

The scary part was that I didn't know exactly what I wanted the rumor to be.

Chapter
9

Mrs. Westland, you're probably reading this now and I can see your curls bouncing side to side as you shake your head. In my defense, what did I know? I knew Jake Darrow made me melt like a Popsicle on a summer day, that's what. And frankly, that's all that mattered.

But not to worry, you'll be relieved to know that, after getting in the fight, Jake took me home, gave me a brief kiss on the cheek, and told me to call him if I was still interested in a relationship. Instead, I proceeded to go underground.

Friday night, a week later, and I hadn't heard anything from Jake. I still hadn't decided what to do about him. Thoughts swirled around in my head. Every time I thought I could take a chance and call Jake, my mother's words would pop into my mind. Or I'd remember Peter pawing me my freshman year or Mr. Cooper's smarmy stare.

I felt like hitting someone. The only time I ever hit anybody was in sixth grade. Kenny Sommers just wouldn't stop calling me "Chesty." We were on the school playground. I don't even remember hitting him, even though I gave him a nosebleed. I remember my hands curling up, as I tried to keep the anger inside.

The next thing I knew, I was standing over Kenny, watching the blood gush onto his shirt. The playground supervisor didn't wait to hear my side. I got "It's only a nickname, dear," as I was marched to the principal's office. Only a name, all right—one that hurt just as much as any punch.

I pictured Jake and me. We made out like crazy, my tiny little mind reminded me over and over. As if I could forget. I had a sneaking suspicion that I'd hurt Jake's feelings when I pushed him away. But I pushed him away before I did something I would have regretted. Or maybe I wouldn't have regretted it.

I tried to imagine what it would be like to date Jake with gorgeous Savannah Robins lurking in the background, just waiting for him to get tired of me.

I was working the closing shift at the Palace. Susi and I worked that night, but she found an awful lot to do in the immediate vicinity of the manager's office. Moldy Dave was the chef, which didn't tempt any customers our way, let me tell you.

I was left alone to brood about the state of my love life. I hadn't seen or heard from Jake in almost a week, since we'd had our first, and maybe last, date. I'd traded a couple of shifts to avoid him. Maybe he'd done the same to avoid me.

It was getting complicated with Jake. I thought I knew him. I mean, we've been in school together for years and he hung out with my big brothers so much that he practically lived at my house.

I snapped out of my Jake-induced funk and hustled the last few customers out the door. It was closing time, but Mr. Cooper and Susi were nowhere to be found.

"You go ahead, Megan." I jumped at Moldy Dave's voice. I hadn't even heard him walk up to the waitress station. "I still have to finish cleaning the fryer. I'll lock up."

I didn't want to go hunt for Mr. Cooper to ask permission. I had a sneaking suspicion I knew what (or should I say who) he was doing. My nerves jumped at the thought of the lonely walk to my car, but Dave said he'd watch me from the back door.

I punched out and walked warily to my car. Every shadow became a potential mugger and every sound a victim's scream.

The Beast, thankfully, was parked under a streetlight. Moldy Dave's presence in the doorway comforted me.

As I drove off, I breathed a sigh of relief. The imaginary criminals receded.

My mind strayed to Jake's closed face when I ended our date. Would Jake wait long enough for me to figure out my own feelings? Would he give up and move on? Why was I doing this? It was a question I couldn't answer. Or wouldn't answer, a little voice said. I told my tricky subconscious to shut up. I didn't know how I felt about Jake.

I drove to Jilly's. I had to talk to her.

Jilly was home when I got there, thank god. She took one look at my face and put her arms around me and led me inside. While I called my parents to let them know I was at Jilly's, she made me hot chocolate, liberally spiked with booze.

"What's wrong? What happened on your date with Jake?"

"I don't know. Not much happened." I was pretty sure I'd screwed things up with him.

"Maybe I shouldn't tell you this, especially after the day you've had, but Butterball has been talking trash about you and Jake."

"What kind of trash is she spewing now?"

"She said she saw you and Jake making out."

"She did not see us when we were making out, she saw us when we were arguing."

Sure enough, Jilly pounced. "What do you mean, she didn't see you when you were making out?"

I couldn't take it any longer. I had to talk to Jilly about what had been driving me crazy the last few days.

"We went out, but I think we're over already."

"Megan, leave it to you to dump a guy before you even really start going out with him."

"Hey, I thought you didn't like Jake," I said.

"That's when he had a steady girlfriend. Now he's available. Tell me everything."

"Besides, I didn't dump him. Not really. I just don't know if we'll get together again."

"Megan, the guy acts like you're some kind of goddess, and you don't know if you want to go out with him again?"

"I don't know."

"I think you should quit being so chicken and go for it. What do you have to lose?"

We continued talking, but Jilly's words stayed in the back of my mind. Why *did* I push Jake away before we'd even started getting close? *Scaredy cat,* my little voice whispered. Jilly was right, I was a chicken.

After we had exhausted the subject of Jake and me, we stayed up until almost three, drinking spiked hot chocolates and goofing off, until I worked up the nerve to tell Jilly what I wanted to do. "I need your help. I want to get something taken care of Monday. Surgery, but I don't want my parents to know."

"I just wish you'd told me when it happened." Jilly stared down at her hands. "I'm not trying to talk you out of your choice, but I didn't even know you had . . ." her voice trailed off.

My god. Jilly thought I wanted to go to a clinic or something.

"Jilly," I said, "When would I have had the time for that?

You know I'm still a virgin, for god's sake. I want to have cosmetic surgery."

The relief in her face was obvious. Jilly knew that I'd considered surgery and she knew about my secret boob-job savings. But I think she expected me to do it later, like after college. It's not that I don't trust Jilly. I do. I didn't say anything, because I wasn't sure I wanted to go through with it. Jilly thinks I'm fine the way I am, but hey, she's my best friend, it's almost a requirement.

Have you ever seen those mother/daughter look-alike photos? You know, the ones where everybody oohs and ahs over how similar-looking the mother and daughter are. My mother and I are nothing alike. My mom's tiny, my grandmother is flat, so imagine my family's surprise when their fifth-grade darling grew breasts the size of watermelons.

I'm sure my mom didn't know what to do, but neither did I. She took a little too long to take me to buy a bra and I was too embarrassed to ask. My face still burns when I think about the teasing I endured until Mom finally got a clue.

Jilly and I had had a few in-depth discussions about the way I felt about my chest and all those times she stood up for me in elementary school, the times when the boys were snapping my bra strap. I knew she understood how much the teasing hurt me. She'd rip into anybody she heard making a rude comment. So she wasn't completely surprised when I asked her to come with me to the plastic surgeon's.

"Megan, I know people rag on you about your chest, but this is a big step."

"Do you remember that time when Stephanie was drunk and she told me my hooters were getting huge?"

"Vaguely."

"Do you remember what else she said? She said it must be because I was letting all the boys rub them. Jilly, I was twelve when she said that."

"God, Megan! I'm sorry."

"It's not your fault you have a bitchy stepmom. I want to get rid of them. I want to look normal."

Jilly tapped my arm. "You do look normal, Megan. Don't you know the girls in our class would kill for a figure like yours?"

The hot chocolate à la Jilly was kicking in and I was feeling no pain. "Good. They can have them when I'm done. I'll auction them off."

We giggled like idiots until we fell asleep.

We got up bright and early the next day. Technically, I hadn't exactly talked to my parents about this. Technically, I would have to forge the permission paperwork they had faxed over to Jilly's dad's home office. Technically, I'd probably be grounded for months after the surgery.

The appointment was for Monday morning. I didn't have to work that day and Jilly asked Susi to cover her shift. There were some perks to being the owner's daughter.

I swallowed hard, and reminded myself it was just a consultation, the first step. I could change my mind anytime. That didn't comfort me at all. I bit my nails the entire trip to Des Moines.

Dr. Bernard's assistant had me fill out a ton of paperwork, sniffing suspiciously, I thought, at the signed permission slip I handed her. She led me to the exam room, where she instructed me to undress from the waist up before she swept from the room. I waited, hanging in the breeze in my hospital gown.

The actual consultation wasn't bad at all. Dr. Bernard turned out to be a short redhead wearing a Counting Crows T-shirt under her lab coat. She also, I noted, had no chest to speak of. It amazed me that she empathized with my problem.

We went over my surgical options. I must admit it freaked me out a little when she took a marker to my breasts and diagrammed where she'd be slicing and dicing.

"I'll be honest with you. You have a borderline problem. The weight of your breasts will cause you some discomfort during your life and your posture needs work."

I was surprised she labeled my gigantic breasts as "borderline." Something of what I was feeling must have shown in my face.

"I know it's hard for you to believe right now, but you are fine just the way you are."

She watched my face. "In fact, I have patients who pay me to make their breasts look exactly like yours."

I laughed at the thought. Who would pay to look like me?

The doctor continued, "I would hate to see you make a decision like this so soon. What do your parents think about all this?"

I gulped. I felt like I had a mouthful of sand. "They just want me to be happy."

"Megan, I want you to think about this before you go forward with the surgery. And next time, bring your parents." Her voice was stern. "And at the very least, please talk to them about this. Cosmetic surgery isn't a decision you should be making alone."

I hung my head. *Busted.* I suppressed an inappropriate giggle. If Dr. Bernard's nurse held a grudge and called my parents or something, I'd be busted and *busted.* My parents would never let me have the surgery if they found out that I'd already gone behind their backs. I felt bad about lying, but I was desperate.

"I'll talk to my parents, I promise." I couldn't imagine what they'd say, but I would talk to them. If they said no, I'd just have to wait until I was eighteen.

"If they approve and you're sure, we'll schedule the surgery. Your parents can call my assistant to make the arrangements."

I had a lot to think about on the ride home. Jilly was quiet, too.

"I want you to know I'll be there either way, Megan, but I think you're gorgeous the way you are, inside and out."

"Thanks, Jilly. Thanks for being there for me today."

I gave her a hug and walked up to my house, wishing the whole time that I could see myself the way Jilly did.

Chapter

10

Mrs. Westland, have you ever had one of those
weeks? When nothing seems to make sense and
everybody's acting weird? That's the kind of week
I had.

I was surprised when Jake called the next day and apologized. He sounded so sweet.

That night, Jake picked me up at my house. My brothers
were harassing him, as usual, when my parents decided to get
in on the let's-embarrass-Megan's-date act.

My hand was on the door to freedom when I heard my
mom call my name. Mom had been giving me the silent
treatment since our fight, and I figured I'd better not act
selectively deaf. Jake took my hand and we walked into the
living room where my parents were watching a Disney movie
with the little guys.

"Where are you kids off to?" my mother asked, sugar-
sweet.

"To a movie," I replied.

"I made the boys' favorite dinner tonight. I wish they would tell me when they have other plans," my mom said, ignoring Jake's hand entwined in mine.

"No, Mom. It's just Jake and me tonight."

The expression on my mom's face was almost comical. My dad shot her a warning look and she managed to keep her mouth closed.

"Have a good night, Meg." My dad was the only person I ever let call me that. It reminds me of when he used to read *Little Women* to me. I could feel my mom's frown at my back as we left.

We met Jilly and Lyle for dinner before the movie. We'd agreed on the Cyclone Pub, near the university. Jilly and Lyle were already sitting at a cozy booth by the window. We slid into the booth and said our hellos.

Jake and Jilly were debating the merits of which movie to see, a horror flick (Jilly) or a romantic comedy (Jake). Jilly's choice didn't surprise me in the least, because she's an absolute ghoul when it comes to entertainment, but I have to admit I was a little startled by Jake's.

Jilly kept staring at something or someone in the corner of the restaurant. I caught her eye and I gave her a *what's up?* look. Jilly motioned in the direction of the counter. Susi Fielding sat at a stool alone, wearing a tight black mini and, if possible, an even tighter red T-shirt.

"There's Susi. I'm going to ask her to join us," I said. Susi looked like somebody who had been waiting a long time. Maybe she'd been stood up.

"Hey, Susi, how's it going?"

She turned around. "Oh, hi, Megan, what are you doing here?" Her red T-shirt was emblazoned with *Pancake Palace Royals*.

"We're having dinner and then going to a movie. Want to join us?" I said quickly.

"No thanks. I'm meeting someone." She didn't elaborate.

I said good-bye and returned to the booth. When we left for the movie, Susi was still alone at the counter.

After the movie, we said good-bye to Jilly and Lyle, who had alone-time on their minds just as much as Jake and I did.

"Want to come over to my house?"

I hesitated. I'd met Jake's parents at football games and stuff, but this was different.

"My parents are in Des Moines at a concert."

"Sure."

We headed to his house. I'd never been to Jake's house before, but I didn't get much time to check it out. Somehow, we were on the couch before I knew it, indulging in marathon kissing. Jake's hands wandered a little too close to my not-so-prized possessions. I panicked and pulled away. What was Jake really after in this relationship? Did he know anything about the real me?

"What's wrong?" Jake asked. He sounded irritated.

"Let me catch my breath, okay?" I said.

We sat in silence for a moment.

"Jake, what color are my eyes?"

"Huh?" he said brilliantly.

"You've known me since we were little kids. My brothers are your best friends. We're dating. It's not beyond the realm of possibility that you would know the color of my eyes."

I was steamed. None of the other boys I had dated, including my former steady Sam, knew what color my eyes were because they were too busy staring at my overdeveloped body. But I thought Jake was different.

"I think they're blue."

"You *think* they're blue." I know Jake could tell I was mad, but I was really hurt, too. I had been stupid to think he could see beyond the breasts.

"Take me home," I snapped.

"I'll take you home, but I have something to tell you first," Jake snapped back. What did he have to be pissed about?

"What?" I said.

"I'm color-blind. I don't know what color your eyes are because I'm color-blind. I couldn't ask Dennis or David, not then and not now. They'd never let me hear the end of it."

I was such an idiot.

"Jake, I'm sorry."

"Megan, can't you try to trust me, just a little? If all I was after was sex, I could have just stayed with Savannah."

"Oh. Oh, I hadn't realized that you two had—" I sputtered to a stop. Don't ask me why, but it hadn't occurred to me that Jake and Savannah had been together that way. Naïve, I know.

"Did you love her?" I asked.

There was a long silence. "No."

That revelation was pretty much a mood killer, so Jake drove me home in silence.

My week just kept getting better and better, Mrs. Westland. I was at work and I'd just been stiffed on not one, but two tables. To make matters worse, Jake's parents came in and were sitting in my section. I got the feeling they were checking me out. I eyed the table nervously. They were sitting at a four-top, and there were two extra menus next to the placemats.

Jake was working, too, so he came out to say hello to his parents. It was slow in the kitchen (big surprise), so he pulled up a chair. I was uncomfortable the minute he introduced us.

"Mom, Dad, this is Megan. Megan, these are my parents." Jake's voice sounded like he was introducing me to the Queen of England or something.

Mr. Darrow, his eyes the same chocolate-chip brown as

Jake's, twinkled a hello. His mom, a tiny brunette, just wanted to let me know how welcome I wasn't in Jake's life.

Mrs. Darrow said, "It's nice to meet you, Marcy."

At first I thought she was just a little absentminded, until she repeatedly talked about Savannah whenever I was in earshot. The way this evening was going, I thought that maybe they'd invited Savannah to dinner or something.

The next time I checked on Jake's parents, Mr. Cooper was sitting at the table. Next to him was a woman I assumed was his wife. I could hear her jangle as she moved and I noticed a dozen or so cheap crosses draped around her neck.

Mr. Cooper said hello in a voice so quiet I almost didn't recognize him. His wife had a voice like the buzz of a mosquito.

Mrs. Darrow called me "Marcy," no matter how many times Jake corrected her.

I finally got the hint when she said, "Jake hasn't mentioned a young lady since his girlfriend Savannah left for her grandparents' last month. She'll be home soon."

"*Ex*-girlfriend, Mom. You know that."

Jake's mom made it clear, all very subtly, of course, that she wanted Jake to get back together with Savannah; then she asked me where I went to church.

"My family doesn't go to church." The minute I said it, I knew I'd said the wrong thing. How could she not know that, anyway? Dennis and David were Jake's best friends.

At my response, Mrs. Darrow made a little face at her hus-band, which went undetected by the rest of the table, but not by me. But maybe that was the point. Jake went back to the grill and I went to wait on other customers.

Later, while the rest of the group had coffee, I cleared the table. Unfortunately, Mr. Cooper decided to be helpful. So helpful, he followed me to the dishwasher and put his hand on my ass when my hands were full of plates.

"Mr. Cooper, leave me alone. Leave me alone, or else." I whispered it as I threw an anxious look toward the door. What would Jake think if he saw this? Or his mom? She'd probably think it was my fault.

"Or else what? You'll tell your new boyfriend?" The mild-mannered man who meekly *yes dear* and *no dear*-ed his wife was gone. In his place was a frothing-at-the- mouth sex fiend. I noticed he kept his voice low enough that it wouldn't carry into the other room.

"Big deal," he continued. "Boys like Jake want only one thing from a girl like you."

There it was again, that horrible phrase. I carefully put down the plate I carried. It wouldn't do to bust up the restau-rant's china. Mr. Cooper would just take it out of my pay-check. My fists clenched. I ached to punch Mr. Cooper in his hypocritical, hymn-singing mouth.

"If you don't leave me alone, I'll tell your wife," I hissed and headed for the safety of the waitress station. If that didn't make him leave me alone, nothing would.

"Why, Marcy, you're a little flushed," Mrs. Darrow said, when I returned with the check.

I didn't even bother to correct her.

The Beast was acting up again, so Jake gave me a ride home. On the way, he apologized for the way his mom acted, but for some reason, it didn't help.

I gave him a brief kiss and said good night. The next day, I called in sick to work. Okay, I admit it. I just stayed in bed and felt sorry for myself. But can you blame me?

Chapter

11

Mrs. Westland, it's never good when a guy wants to talk. A few nights later, Jake came by my house "to talk." They never want to talk, at least not any guys I know. "Talk" is guy-speak for "dump."

We drove to the pool parking lot. Jake probably didn't want my nosy brothers watching. Neither did I. He probably didn't want to tell them he was dumping me already. I probably didn't want them to see me cry.

Jake and I sat on the hood of his car and stared up at the moon.

"I'm sorry I haven't called you." Jake seemed to be memorizing the clouds and all the constellations.

I did a little stargazing myself. "It's okay. I'm sure you were . . . busy."

"No, I wasn't—I mean—I should have called."

"Jake, maybe we should just . . . forget about . . . everything. You just broke up with Savannah and this is a bad time to—start anything new."

"Why don't you trust me? The first time we seem to be getting closer, you pull away." Anger made his voice low and flat.

For a minute, I thought of Sam's betrayal, but then a picture of Jake patiently teaching me how to swing a bat flashed in my mind. They weren't anything alike.

I knew what Jake was saying was true. Somehow, I thought it'd be all better after I got the boob job. Being with him now was too confusing.

"Megan, it's just that . . . I'm confused." Jake was a mind reader. What chance did our relationship have if we both were confused?

"Jake, I'll clear it up for you. You just broke up with your girlfriend, your mom can't even remember my name, and one of your dad's buddies tried to grope me."

"What? Megan—"

But I didn't wait to explain. "Let's avoid each other until you leave for college. It shouldn't be too hard. It's only for a few weeks." I hopped off the hood and stomped off. Jake didn't follow me.

Jilly's house was only a block away. I'd call my parents and ask to spend the night with her. Unfortunately, she wasn't home. Probably out with Lyle. I stomped off the front porch. I'd go for a walk until I could go home. One look at my face and Dennis and David would be pestering me to find out what was wrong.

As I walked, the rage bubbled inside me. I hated what was happening in my life. I thought about my conversation with Jake. I didn't even get to tell him about Mr. Cooper.

I asked myself why, out of all the girls in town, I was being harassed. But then I saw my breasts bobbing up and down. And I knew. The object of every leering glance, of every rude comment, the source of all my problems was held in place by a white cotton bra. I decided to call Dr. Bernard as soon as I could.

When I got home, I had a message from Brent. Dennis had taken it down. I recognized his sloppy scrawl. He drew little kisses and hearts all over the paper. He thought he was so funny.

There was also a message from Mr. Cooper that there was a softball game tomorrow night at seven p.m. Jeesh! He was taking this restaurant softball tournament thing totally seriously.

Great. I called Jilly. She was finally home, but sounded distracted.

"Jilly, what's the matter?"

"Megan, don't get mad, okay?"

"Whenever someone says that to me, it's almost a guarantee that I'm going to get majorly pissed."

"Butterball called me right before you and pretended to be all concerned about you because you were seeing Jake. But she really just wanted to tell me that he's only dating you to get some."

"If you talk to Butterball again, tell her to mind her own business." I tried to keep my voice light, but my voice trembled.

"If it's any comfort, I don't think it's true. Jake cares about you. I know you're scared, but you have to take a chance sometime."

"Listen, Jake is a nonissue. Pick me up tomorrow night and you can lecture me about my imaginary sex life then. I've got to call Brent."

I hung up the phone to the sound of Jilly's gasp of surprise. Jilly would be burning rubber to get over here and would be too distracted by the Brent thing to interrogate me about Jake.

It's not that I couldn't tell Jilly. I've told her my deepest, darkest secret. It's just my head was still spinning from all the hot/cold from Jake. Okay, maybe it was me blowing hot/cold. I was too confused to know.

I picked up the phone. "Hey, Brent, it's me, Megan."

"Hi, Meggie." I winced. I hated it when people called me that. "Want to go to a movie tomorrow night?" The hope in his voice made my stomach churn.

"No, I can't." There was silence on the other end of the line. I'd hurt his feelings. Now I was taking it out on Brent, a totally nice guy. But he wasn't Jake.

I forged ahead. "Jilly and I are both playing on Pancake Palace's softball team. There's a game tomorrow night."

"Oh, okay. I'd better let you go then."

"Wait, Brent, do you want to come and watch? I know it's lame, but maybe we could hang out afterward."

"That'd be great, Meggie. I can't wait to see you!"

After getting the details of when and where for the big game against Tony's Truck Stop, Brent hung up. But I sat staring at the phone, wondering what I'd gotten myself into.

When Jilly picked me up, I filled her in that I'd finally agreed to go out with Brent. I expected her to shatter my eardrums screaming her approval, but she didn't. Instead, she kept checking to see if I was okay. She actually pulled the car over and sat there, her hands twisting and untwisting on the steering wheel.

"What about Jake?"

I looked at her in amazement. "Jilly, it's just a date. Jake and I aren't exclusive."

"Megan, you've had exactly one boyfriend the entire time I've known you. And plenty of guys have been interested, believe me. You practically gagged every time I mentioned Brent. I'm just a little confused."

I doubted that Jilly would have been excited to know that I said yes to Brent to try to get back at Jake. I know I wasn't too excited that I'd done such a cruddy thing.

We finally got to the playing field. As Jilly locked her car, she turned to me and said, "You looked pretty tight with Jake the other night. Why are you going out with Brent tonight?"

Good question, huh, Mrs. Westland? I'd been asking myself the same thing ever since I said yes to Brent. Which reminded me, where was Brent?

I scanned the crowd as we walked by the bleachers. There were actually a few spectators already there, but I didn't see Brent. Jilly waved to her loyal Lyle, who was already sitting in the bleachers with his friend Kevin.

Susi and Mr. Cooper were over by the dugout. As I watched, Mr. Cooper inched closer. He said something to Susi and stalked off. God, I needed to talk to Susi. What the hell was she thinking?

More importantly, what was Mr. Cooper thinking? I mean, he was supposed to be the adult. What he was thinking about was statutory rape. Susi looked as street-smart as Madonna, but she was seventeen.

Before I could track her down, my pulse let off a series of blips, as if I had some kind of radar, letting me know Jake was in the near vicinity. Sure enough, he jogged over to us.

"Hi. Are you ready for the game?" He aimed the question at both of us.

Then in a soft, urgent voice, he asked, "Megan, can I talk to you later? Maybe after the game?"

Before I could answer, Brent came racing over. "Megan, sorry I'm late. I'll make it up to you after the game. How about if we go to the St. Regis?" he added.

I'm sure you've been there, Mrs. Westland, that fancy place by the college. Not exactly a normal first date for teenagers. Brent was trying to impress me.

***

I knew I was making a horrible mistake going out with him, but what could I do? I couldn't answer him. Jake acted like he'd just caught a whiff of one of Moldy Dave's pet projects.

We all stood there with nobody saying a word. Brent waited for an answer. Jilly's head bobbed back and forth between Jake and Brent, like she was watching a tennis match. Jake shot the evil eye at Brent, and Brent kept smiling, without a clue.

Me? I sweated, especially when Jake shot the evil whammy my way. Like he had anything to be mad about. I felt like sticking my tongue out at him. Mr. Confused. Luckily, I guess, the opposing team showed up to divert our attention.

Tony's Truck Stop. I'm guessing a little steroid guzzling didn't faze these guys one bit. A bunch of beefy, postadolescent jocks piled out of a variety of pickups, carrying their equipment and several twelve-packs. They had actual uniforms and brand-new bats and gloves. And bad attitudes.

It was almost game time, so Brent left for the bleachers and Jilly, Jake, and I went to warm up with the rest of the Pancake Palace team. By the first inning, it was clear Tony's Truck Stop played to win. Whatever it took.

Mr. Cooper handed out Pancake Palace T-shirts. I checked the size on mine, but I had grabbed the last shirt. Mr. Cooper had given Jilly and me the *exact* same size.

Mrs. Westland, do I look like I wear a size small??

Mr. Cooper was more of a perv than I had suspected. There was no way I was asking Jake, and I was too embarrassed to ask anyone else. I decided to wear it and hope no one would notice.

Still, everything went fairly well, until it was my turn at bat. I nervously tugged at my shirt, feeling it stretch tightly across my chest. Bad move.

When I walked to the mound, Tony's Truck Stop started the catcalls, the whistles, and the comments.

Mrs. Westland, have you ever thought about what it's like for me? Most people, girls especially, think it'd be so great to have large breasts. Wrong. Most guys don't even see me, they only see my cup size.

I stood there, face burning, and hoped the ref or Mr. Cooper or somebody would help. Stop the game or something. Nothing. I could hear Jilly and Jake and some of my other teammates telling me to ignore them.

The pitcher wound up. First strike. More whistles. I could feel sweat trickle down between my breasts.

While the pitcher got ready to throw his next pitch, I thought about it. I knew that even if someone came to my rescue, it wouldn't really stop.

I shut out the noise from the other team and concentrated on my stance and grip, just like Jake had shown me. When the next pitch came, I swung with all my might, putting all my anger into it. To be honest, I was hoping I'd hit the crudest Truck Stop player, ol' Tony himself, right in the balls. Instead, I hit a home run.

What a feeling! First I was so amazed, I just stood there as the ball soared over the fence. Then I ran, not even caring who watched my chest bounce up and down.

And when I rounded home, Jake was there. He picked me up and twirled me around as the rest of the Pancake Palace team cheered. The opposing team grumbled and bitched, but didn't have much to say during my remaining turns at bat.

I didn't hit any more home runs, but it was a great game. We won by two runs and it was our first victory. A victory for me, too.

Everyone on the team was excited. After the game was over and the other team left to drown their sorrows, we all stood laughing and joking. Even Mr. C.

"Let's go to the restaurant to celebrate." There were a few moans. "I'm buying," Mr. Cooper added. We all cheered. Then I remembered my date with Brent.

"Brent, would it be all right if we—?"

"Pancake Palace it is," he said, smiling. I knew he was a little disappointed, but he was too polite to say anything.

I rode with Brent to the Palace. Almost everyone on the team was there. They were gathered around a huge booth. Brent and I sat down next to Jilly and Lyle. I tried not to be obvious with Brent sitting right next to me. But I hate to admit it, I checked to see if Jake was there. Nope.

Mr. Cooper and Susi were missing, too.

I should have said something then and there, but, Mrs. Westland, I had too much going on at the time.

"After this, let's all go over to my house to celebrate Megan's home run and our victory against Tony's Truck Stop," Jilly said to the whole table. I thought a party might take my mind off Jake. I'd have fun with Brent and forget about Jake Darrow.

Susi slipped in a few minutes later. Soon after, Mr. Cooper bustled to the table with a huge order of appetizers. He set the first plate down and reached for the second.

I met his eyes levelly and leaned in to tap his smudged collar. "New shade for your wife, huh, Mr. Cooper?" He blanched and almost dropped a plate of potato skins.

That's when Jake showed up with Savannah.

Chapter 12

Mrs. Westland, I'd like to say it was Moldy Dave reaching for the appetizers with his long, greasy hands that made me lose my appetite. You never know where his hands have been. But, in reality, it was the sight of Savannah hanging on Jake's arm that made me want to hurl.

To make matters worse, they sat down straight across from me. Savannah smirked at me as she snuggled up to Jake. She'd never paid any attention to me before. I was betting that someone had told her about Jake and me. She acted so damn smug. My hands itched for a sharp steak knife.

I kept my head down and tried to have a good time.

Jilly kicked me under the table every five minutes, but I ignored her signal for a little confab and kept my attention on my date.

Nobody seemed too surprised to see Jake and Savannah together. Except me. Of course, *surprised* doesn't exactly describe it. Maybe "knife to the heart"?

They probably never broke up, I sneered to myself. Jake's supposed infatuation with me cleared up mighty quickly. Who was I to talk? I was already on a date with Brent. So I smiled and laughed and pretended I was having the best time.

My acting skills must have been substandard, because eventually Brent leaned over. "Megan, are you okay? You're a little pale."

Brent was truly concerned. It made me feel guilty, so, of course, I acted like a total bitch.

"I'm *fine*," I practically snarled. His puppy-dog eyes made me feel worse.

I tried to soften my tone. "I'll go splash a little water on my face. Maybe my first home run tired me out," I joked weakly.

I stood up. Jilly got up to follow, but I signaled her back with a short shake of my head. I didn't feel like hashing it out with her right that second.

I left the table and headed for the bathroom. I needed a breather anyway. Jake was getting on my nerves. And I'd noticed Savannah hadn't lightened up on the toxic scent. She was clogging my sinuses.

I splashed water on my face. Great, no paper towels. I blotted my face with some toilet paper and forced myself to breathe deeply. I decided that, judging from the bathroom mirror, it was totally believable to tell Brent I didn't feel well and wanted to go home. I squared my shoulders and walked back into battle.

It wasn't a complete shock when I saw Jake leaning up against a wall near the phones.

"Megan, can I talk to you? Savannah just showed up at my house tonight—"

"Save it, Jake." I stalked back to the table, Jake right behind me.

More of the Pancake Palace team had showed up. The appetizers had been hoovered and everyone munched on burgers and fries. Brent was intent on a conversation with Susi. Mr. Cooper bustled up with another huge tray of food. Boy, he was being generous. I wondered who he was trying to impress.

Mr. Cooper shot me a dirty look and I smiled sweetly. I wanted him to know that he wasn't getting away with what he was doing to Susi. Even if I was just a kid, I knew the law.

My gaze drifted over to Susi. I was worried about her. She seemed to ignore Mr. C. altogether, although her voice got a little louder and more animated each time he came to the table with more soda or fries or dessert. You'd think we'd just won the World Series the way he fed us.

I cleared my throat and prepared to make my excuses and go home and crawl in a hole or something.

"I think we'll skip the party tonight." My voice came out as a sort of croak.

"Aren't you feeling well?" Savannah's voice sounded as sweet as the maple syrup we served and about as natural.

"I have class tomorrow."

"Class, in the summer?" The pitying tone in Savannah's voice made it clear to everyone that she thought I was a total nerd.

"On second thought, we will go."

Unbelievable. Now I couldn't just get out of this nightmare evening gracefully. Savannah was really rubbing it in, in that sneaky way that boys never caught. I wanted to go home and eat a pound or two of chocolate. Instead, Brent and I headed to Jilly's. I just prayed Jake would get a clue and take his girl-friend home or back to Arizona or something.

Jilly's little get-together had the potential of a full-force rager. There were cars parked all over her street. We could hear the music blaring as we pulled up. I tried not to flinch when Brent's hand touched mine. It wasn't *his* hand I wanted to be holding.

Most of the party was outside, so we walked around to the backyard. It was barely dark, my favorite time, especially in summer. The sky was a dreamy purple. The smell of the corn in nearby fields tinged the air with a sharp green scent.

An impromptu dance floor had been set up by the pool. Brent pulled me out to the dance floor and into his arms. A slow song played. There was no sign of Jake. Maybe my date with Brent wouldn't be so bad after all, though I knew I wouldn't want another one. I felt content to be dancing under the night sky.

At least I did, until Jake tapped Brent on the shoulder like in some old movie and asked to cut in. Brent graciously went over to talk to Jilly and Lyle. They all watched Jake and me from a cluster of lounge chairs.

"What do you want, Jake?" I fought against inhaling the clean crisp scent of him. I wanted to touch his hair, his lips, but I didn't. Instead of answering me, Jake drew me close. As we danced, my head touched his shoulder, even as I told myself that's not where it should be. Not where I should be.

I could see Brent over Jake's shoulder. He looked like a kid who had lost his favorite toy. I knew how he felt. It's the way I felt when Jake showed up with Savannah.

"I'm sorry, Megan."

"For what? I don't own you. As a matter of fact, I thought Savannah was the only one who could legitimately claim that honor."

"God, Megan . . ." he trailed off. I walked away. I didn't want to hear what excuses he had. I didn't deserve to be in the middle of some weird game. I wouldn't be treated like that.

As I stalked away, I noticed Susi, sitting alone, lost in thought. I got the feeling she would have avoided me if she'd seen me coming sooner.

"Hi, Susi."

"Hi, Megan." Susi kept her eyes lowered. I sat down next to her on the lawn chair.

"Susi, what's up with you and Mr. Cooper?" Silence.

"You know he's married—"

Susi interrupted me. "He loves me. You don't know what he says to me in private."

I couldn't believe what I was hearing. I could only imagine what he said to Susi. I repressed a shudder. He'd tried some pretty cheesy lines on me. But how could I tell her that?

I tried again. "Susi, I know it's none of my business, but—"

"No, it's not any of your business, Megan." Without a backward glance, Susi moved away.

I sighed and walked to where Brent still stood.

"Brent, would you mind if we left? I'm . . . just not in the right mood for a party."

He gazed at me for a long moment and nodded. As we left the party, I felt Jake's eyes boring into my back.

On the way home, we were both quiet. Brent cleared his throat. "Megan, if you would have told me about you and Jake Darrow, I wouldn't have kept asking you out."

"Brent, you're a nice guy. It's complicated with Jake, that's all. We're really just friends."

As the words left my mouth, I felt as though "fraud" suddenly appeared on my forehead. In glowing pink neon.

Mrs. Westland, have you ever had to let someone down gently? Well, then, you know there's no such thing.

I could see it in Brent's eyes. He thought I was BS-ing him.

I could maybe keep on BS-ing myself, but I couldn't keep doing it to him.

"I'm sorry, Brent. Jake and I are more than friends."

"Yeah, I figured. I could tell by the way he watched you tonight."

"What do you mean?"

"Well, the whole night he ignored Savannah and stared at you. He looked like he wanted to kick my ass or something." Brent trailed off. "Megan, why am I even telling you this?"

"Brent, I know. I'm sorry." That phrase was getting a lot of use.

We reached my house on that last sorry note. Brent walked me to the door and said good night. From the door, I watched him drive away, and I knew it was the last I'd see of him.

What I didn't expect was to see Jake pull up a few minutes later. He must have practically followed us home.

I went outside and waited. I didn't have long to wait. Jake came bounding up the stairs as I sat down on the porch swing.

"Megan, just listen for a minute. Savannah and I are not together. She showed up tonight out of the blue and invited herself along. I told her again that it was over. She just didn't get it, but she does now. You're smart, funny, and beautiful, even if you do confuse the hell out of me most of the time. I want to be with you."

Jake sat next to me and took my hand. "Megan, did you hear me? I want to be with you. Only you."

I couldn't answer him. I was stunned. No wonder Jake kept repeating himself. It was the last thing I was expecting to hear.

"I think I'll make you repeat that a few hundred times more," I said as my lips met his.

Chapter
13

Mrs. Westland, I was working the closing shift at the Palace. For once, I was actually working it. I didn't mind, since I needed the money. It was just weird that night.

Jilly, Susi, and I were working. Moldy Dave went to the back to do some prep work around eight. Then Mr. Cooper sent Susi to make the bank deposit. A minute or two later, he told Jilly she could leave in an hour if it didn't get any busier, and he slipped out the door. After Jilly closed her jaw, she punched out. She wanted to stick around to help me close, but I told her to go enjoy her Friday night with Lyle.

While alone, I brooded about what to do about my breast reduction. I still hadn't talked to my parents. Hadn't even mentioned it.

To add to my troubles, Peter Fenton walked in about nine o'clock. He took his sweet time—even ordering a dessert. It was closing time when I reluctantly locked the front door behind the last coffee drinker. Peter and I were alone in the dining room.

Peter made me a little nervous. This was the first time I'd been alone with him since the scene at the Pit. At least Moldy Dave was in the back somewhere.

I didn't want him getting the idea I was tonight's chef's special. I pointedly brought him his check, but he just leaned back in his booth and gave me a make-me-leave grin.

I vacuumed the room the Kiwanis would be using in the morning, and then worked my way up to the front, near the pie case. When a beefy arm snaked around my waist, I jumped a mile, pivoted, and almost collided with Peter Fenton's blond jock face.

"Peter, cut it out." I shut off the vacuum and gave the cord a tug till it came loose from the socket. No sense in screaming over the roar of the vacuum. I frantically hoped Mr. Cooper would return. Like, immediately.

"Make me." God, what was it with this town? Half the boys I played on the monkey bars with turned out to be rapists or cheats.

"Mr. Cooper will be back any minute."

I could hear my own heartbeat, pounding out *run, run, run!*

I knew Peter was getting off on scaring me.

I tried to squirm out of his grasp, but he was too quick for me. His free hand wormed its way up to the front opening of my uniform.

I'd be damned if I was going to let a two-hundred-pound

gorilla paw me. He expected me to fight. The gleam in his eyes told me he wanted me to fight.

Instead, I reached into the pie case. It confused him for a minute. Long enough for me to grab an open can of whipped cream.

I jabbed the point in the general direction of his piggy little eyes. I felt it connect with something fleshy. I sprayed whipped cream into his eyes. I elbowed him in the stomach for good measure and bolted for the door. Out of the corner of my eye, I saw a figure walking toward the front door.

I fumbled for the key in my pocket and headed for the front. I didn't care who was there; I would welcome them with open arms. I could hear Peter cursing as he came behind me, but I didn't care. He wouldn't do anything with a witness around.

I opened the door and practically fell into Jake's arms. I blurted out the story with Peter grumbling about how I couldn't take a joke. As I talked, Mr. Cooper came in.

Even in the state I was in, I noticed that his tie was askew and his shirt was untucked. His face was red, like he'd been running a race. That was some trip to the bank.

Mr. Cooper and Peter left for the emergency room. Mr. Cooper, creep that he is, believed Peter, who muttered that it was an accident. Mr. Cooper should have given Peter a ride to the police station, not the ER.

Jake had had his arm around me and I hadn't even noticed.

My head was spinning. I couldn't believe Peter had tried something like this.

We drove around until we finally found Fairview's finest, idling at the pool parking lot. Steve Hanover was on duty. He'd graduated six years ago and I felt okay about telling him what had happened.

As we left, Steve put a hand on my shoulder and said, "Be careful. We'll put a little healthy fear into him, but you be careful, Megan."

Steve started to leave but then said, "Let me know if he gives you any more trouble."

After the squad car pulled away, I drew a deep, shaky breath and went into the comfort of Jake's arms.

Mrs. Westland, you don't have to tell me how lucky I was. I know. I had nightmares for weeks afterward.

Jake helped a lot. I always felt safe with him. And it helped that Peter went out of his way to avoid me after that.

The whole thing with Peter had my mom scared. I told her about it because I knew if I didn't, someone else would. She still gave me a hard time about curfews, but she smiled at Jake once in a while.

I didn't want to spoil the little time we had left together. Before I knew it, summer would be over. Being part of a couple again was a weird experience for me. Jake called me every night. We tried to ignore the ticking college time bomb, but it was in the back of both our minds. Jake would be leaving for some stupid college on the West Coast. Also known as Stanford.

And my brothers weren't making it easy on us, either. Every time Jake came over to pick me up, they started in.

"We wondered what was up when we came home and caught you and Jake in the hammock making out. Megan's shirt was unbuttoned." That was Dennis.

I blushed as red as Jilly's convertible. "My shirt was not unbuttoned, you moron."

"It won't be, either," Jake told them, as he took my hand to guide me away from my idiotic brothers, who had actually managed to embarrass him. "We'll be late for the movies. Are you ready?"

I was ready. In more ways than one. We'd been spending every minute in virtual lip-lock. Jake and I got creative. We found a way to be together, even at work. Pancake Palace had a basement storage room that had long been the topic of speculation and rumor.

I now knew some of those rumors were true. The storage room was now our private place—an oasis in the desert of pancakes. A fifteen-minute lull at the Palace and we were down there faster than you could say "two eggs over easy."

I got the feeling Jake was trying to do the honorable thing. Neither of us was happy about it, but it bugged the hell out of me. Two weeks before college and he wanted to keep us firmly at second base. I planned to change that situation no later than our next visit to the storage room. Which was a Friday night. The traditionally slow night at Pancake Palace.

That Friday, I scooted down to the basement as soon as Mr. Cooper was out of sight. I knew Jake would be seconds behind me. No matter what his honorable intentions were, he wanted to go to the basement as badly I did.

The storage room is in the far corner of the basement, and the light's pretty bad. It always smells like stale cheese, but that had never stopped us. It obviously didn't stop someone else, either. The storage room was already occupied. Damn! I had a feeling I knew who was there, but I hoped I was wrong.

Whispers came drifting out to where I stood, too embarrassed to move. A low masculine voice spoke. What I overheard made me blush. I heard Jake's feet as he ran lightly down the stairs.

"What's wrong, Megan? Did I take too long?" Jake's voice seemed to echo, but there was no stopping the two in the storage closet. I put my finger to my lips.

Then I could only shake my head and point. The urgent whispers made it pretty obvious.

"Jake, let's go. Whoever it is won't want us standing here gawking when they come out," I whispered.

"Come on, let's see who it is. Maybe Moldy Dave finally got lucky," he whispered back.

"Leave! Now! We can stand at the top of the stairs if you really want to know." Actually, I wanted to know who it was as much as Jake did, but not for the same reason. If Susi was in trouble, which in my book meant sleeping with Mr. Cooper, I wanted to help her. She needed somebody to be her friend. Maybe that someone could be me. But I couldn't imagine hanging around till they emerged.

Instead of going back to my station, I stood by the ice machine, pretending to fill up a bucket for the nonexistent dinner rush. Jake loitered nearby, polishing the back kitchen's counters till they shone.

When Mr. Cooper came walking up the basement steps, oh so casually, Jake stood there with his mouth open, wiping the same spot about five hundred times. Mr. Cooper didn't acknowledge us; he just walked into his office and slammed the door.

"Who'd do it with Mr. C.?" Jake asked. "Maybe it's Deanna, the hostess?"

"Nah, she has better taste than that," I said.

"You're right. Who could it be?" Jake said.

But I knew. I was too late. I hadn't done anything, said anything, and now it was too late. We were so busy whispering, we almost missed the person who came up those steps next. Susi Fielding, of course.

I smothered a sigh. I think Susi heard me, though, because she gave me a little nod as she wandered to the front, presumably to pour coffee for our only customer. But I think she was a little out of it.

"How can she do that? Have sex with Mr. Cooper? He's, like, forty. And he's married." I stated the obvious.

"Love is a strange thing, Megan. You never know who you're going to fall for." Jake pulled me into his arms and gave me a little hug.

I looked up at him. "Jake, Mr. Cooper's old enough to be her father. And he's her *boss*. I think we should say something to somebody."

"Megan, I know Mr. Cooper is taking advantage of her. But maybe you should talk to Susi before we do anything."

Somehow, I didn't feel like the basement tonight. And neither did Jake.

"Want to get together after work?" he asked.

"Of course." I smiled at him, but I couldn't let the subject drop. "Susi's a minor. Mr. C. is breaking the law."

"Megan, Susi knew what she was doing."

"That doesn't make it right. What are we going to do about it?"

"What can we do about it? C'mon, let's get back to work before Mr. C. fires both of us."

I tossed Jake's question around in my mind the rest of my shift. It was driving me crazy, so after my shift was over, I motioned Jilly over to the break table.

"You'll never believe it," I whispered.

"You saw Susi and Mr. Cooper, huh?"

My mouth dropped. I didn't think she'd ever be able to guess.

"You and Jake aren't the only ones that know about the storage room. I caught them there last week."

"Why didn't you say anything?"

"I didn't say anything because I thought you already knew. I saw you watching them at practice the other day," Jilly said.

Jilly was right. I had known, I was just pretending I didn't.

"Why didn't you tell your dad?"

"Like he'd believe me over Mr. Cooper." Sadly, Jilly was right.

She told me she talked to Susi a few days ago about Mr. Cooper. Susi insisted that they'd live happily ever after. That he'd leave his wife.

I could see Susi now, taking money at the cash register. I wondered what it was like for her. I mean, she had just had sex, in a storage room, for god's sake. Then she went back to waitressing like it was no big deal. How could sex be no big deal?

I didn't want my first time with Jake to be in some place like the storage room at the Pancake Palace. Jake had been doing the honorable thing since we'd been dating, but I was getting impatient.

I knew I wanted Jake to be my first, and I wanted it to be soon.

Chapter

14

Mrs. Westland, a few days later an opportunity presented itself. Jake just didn't know it yet.

I was spending the week at Jilly's. Her dad and stepmom were headed to California for a couple of weeks on business. My mom had wanted Jilly to stay with us, but the little guys were sick, contagious, and even my mom didn't want Jilly to stay alone.

"We might call up your mom, invite her to dinner," Mr. Henderson said jovially, as he loaded the car. I could just imagine what Jilly was feeling. Her dad was going to California, it was summer, he didn't have school as an excuse not to take her, and he still hadn't invited Jilly to come along.

We all knew why, and she was sitting in the passenger's seat, staring at her image in the mirror while she pretended to check her makeup. Mr. Henderson gave Jilly a swift peck on the cheek and opened the car door.

"Dad, could I—" Jilly never finished her sentence. Mr.

Henderson had already put the car in gear, impatient to be off.

I stood there with Jilly as she watched her dad leave with his baby bride, and I wondered if he and the first Mrs. Henderson had ever been in love. Jilly was so down, I wanted to cheer her up. I'd have to modify my plans a little. I thought fast.

"Hey, Jilly Billy, let's do something fun. We can have a dinner party. Call Lyle and invite him over, and I'll call Jake. We'll cook something spectacular."

The last part made Jilly laugh because neither of us can cook. But she went inside to call Lyle. I sat on the front steps, working up enough courage to call Jake.

I don't know why I was so nervous, especially since Jake didn't have a clue what was on my agenda after dinner. I reminded myself that Jake would be in college next week. I trusted him, maybe even loved him. I was ready, I assured myself a few million times.

We talked for over an hour before I could get the nerve to ask him to dinner.

"Hey, Lyle said he'd be over at seven. We need to go to the store right now or else dinner won't be ready on time," Jilly said.

"Jake, I'll see you at seven, okay?" My stomach fluttered as I said it.

Jilly and I decided to drive to the big supermarket in the next town because it had a better selection. We also wanted to see if anyone would sell us a bottle of wine. I tried to give Jilly some money for the dinner, but she insisted on treating.

"Dad left me tons of cash."

We decided on steak, baked potatoes, salad, and garlic bread, none of which were beyond our meager cooking skills. We'd even have Lyle grill the steaks, so that left the simple stuff. We grabbed the food, including a decadent chocolate cake for dessert.

On our way to the checkout, we wandered over to the makeup and beauty aisle.

Jilly gave me a wicked smile. She went over and picked up a couple of boxes of condoms. She added some spermacide gel and topped it off with a birth-control sponge.

"My God, Jilly, I guess you and Lyle have serious plans for this evening."

"Megan, you know I'm on the Pill. This stuff isn't for me." Her eyebrows rose meaningfully.

At first, I didn't get it. Then it hit me. My knees forgot how to work. My plan to lose my virginity didn't seem so appealing.

Birth control. I hadn't even given it a thought. Sex was serious stuff. I felt myself blush and scooped the boxes out of the cart.

Her voice stopped me. "You guys seemed pretty hot and heavy the other night."

I dropped the boxes back into the cart. I hid my face in my

hair. "Nothing's going to happen." I was chickening out fast.

"Well, just in case, why don't you keep some of this stuff in the room you're staying in."

We both dissolved into giggles and went back to the wine case. We grabbed several bottles and then got in line at the checkout. The cashier was a college-aged guy. He didn't ID us, thankfully. "Where's the party?" He winked at me as he rang up the wine.

"Oh, we're just having a small dinner party." I put on my most mature tone.

"Some dinner party." He picked up the box of condoms to scan. I'd forgotten about the condoms.

Jilly laughed so hard she was hiccuping. We paid for our groceries and left, laughing till our sides ached.

We got home and went into the kitchen to put away the groceries. Everything except the birth control. I stood there, undecided, turning a box over and over in my hands.

At almost seventeen, I knew I was one of the few virgins in my classroom—heck, maybe in the whole high school. Jilly grabbed the box out of my hand. "C'mon, we need to get ready."

I wore a short sundress and sandals. "I am ready."

"Oh no, you're not. We're going to get dressed to impress tonight."

When I was heading to the shower, Jilly handed me some totally expensive shower gel. It smelled like honey and sunshine. I shaved my legs carefully, and got out of the shower. I put on my robe, prepared to return to my sundress. It was nowhere to be seen.

I wandered upstairs to Jilly's bedroom. Her room was a tornado of clothing, dresses, skirts; everything piled up. Two curling irons, a hair dryer, and hot rollers were all plugged in. I was surprised that she hadn't blown a fuse.

"Deciding what to wear?"

"No, looking for something for you to wear."

I gave her a grateful smile. "Thanks, Jilly, but none of your clothes will fit me." I felt like one of her magical makeover projects.

"These are Stephanie's. She decided she needed a whole new wardrobe when they were in Paris, so these are her Goodwill donations."

I reached out a hand to touch a silky green evening dress. It was soft as down.

"Maybe that one's a little too dressy. You don't want to make Jake think you're trying too hard."

Jilly had done a complete one-eighty where Jake was concerned. She said, "I figure anyone who gets you all in a tizzy can't be all bad. And Jake does seem to be loyal. Besides, this way at least you'll get it over with."

I didn't ask her what "it" was. I knew. Jilly thought it was totally backward for me to still be a virgin.

"Jilly, can I ask you something?"

"Sure."

"Has Lyle ever been with somebody else? I mean, before?"

"Yep. Once."

"Did he love her?"

"No. I don't think so. They got together at a party."

"Does it bother you? Jake told me that he and Savannah, you know. And that he didn't love her."

"You don't have to love someone to sleep with them. Do you love Jake?"

I didn't know. I just shrugged helplessly.

"Well, that doesn't mean you can't get together, does it? Jake cares about you, that's clear, and you care about him. It's better than having sex with someone you hardly know, at a party, your first time."

She changed the subject. "Which one do you like?"

She held up three summer dresses. The one that caught my eye was plain, but I loved it. The color was unusual, a gray-green mossy color. I took off my robe and pulled it over my head. The dress felt like I was wearing a cloud.

"That's the one." I stared in the mirror. I was still me, but what a me. The dress turned my eyes to a smoky green and my hair a wicked red.

"Okay, put your robe back on. I'm going to do your hair and makeup."

Jilly loved to do everyone's makeup. She originally wanted to go to college to study fashion design, but Lyle put an end to that. In between doing my makeup and curling my hair, Jilly managed to get dressed in a knock-'em-dead black dress. She was curled and made up in ten minutes flat.

I lounged back on her bed, careful not to muss a hair.

"Hey, Megan, don't take this the wrong way, but do you actually know what to do with the stuff I bought?"

"You mean the steaks?" I played dumb. "Well, I know you wash the meat, sprinkle seasoning on them, and throw them on the grill."

"Very funny. You won't be laughing when the condom breaks or comes off."

"I'm not sure if we're going to—" It was too late. She was running downstairs to the basement. I could hear her rummaging around in the guestroom where I was staying.

She came back up the stairs, but instead of coming into the bedroom, she went into the kitchen.

A minute later, she returned with a condom and a banana. Jilly proceeded to roll down the condom over the banana with the deft movements of a scientist.

"Uh, I know you've had a lot of practice with Lyle and all, but where in the hell did you learn this stuff?"

"Don't you remember? Right after Stephanie tricked Dad into marrying her, she gave me quite the little safe-sex lecture."

"Stephanie? Not that I doubt the range of her knowledge in this area, but why did she bother?" Jilly's stepmother was not the sort to show any concern, however convoluted, about Jilly's well-being.

"All I can figure is that she didn't want to be called 'Grandma' prematurely."

"She should have thought of that before she married someone old enough to be her grandpa." Jilly and I cracked up at that one.

The doorbell rang just as Jilly finished her little presentation. She discarded the condom, peeled the banana, and ate it as the doorbell continued to chime. She smoothed one rebel curl back from my forehead and said, "Don't move. It's probably Lyle. I'll get it." She ran out of the room but came back to pop her head in and say, "Don't be nervous."

I could hear voices in the hall, but couldn't hear what they were saying. Probably the usual couple stuff. My mind drifted as I wondered what Jake would think when he saw me.

Jilly came charging back into the room. "Lyle's here, and so is Jake. Oh, wait, put these on, okay?" She scooped up a pair of strappy silver sandals from the floor.

I looked at her suspiciously. "Let me guess: Stephanie wears the same size shoe as I do, too."

"Don't be silly. Stephanie has feet like a mule. These are mine, you and I wear the same size, remember?"

I slipped the silver sandals on and took one last glance in the mirror. A me I didn't recognize stood there, looking better than I thought I'd ever look.

I hugged Jilly and grinned. "It's amazing what an expensive hand-me-down will do."

"Let's go." She tugged at my arm. "You're beautiful. I can't wait to see Jake's face."

"Ready or not," I whispered, as I took a deep breath and we left the room.

Mrs. Westland, someone needs to write an etiquette book for what to do the morning after. I mean, not even Jilly mentioned that we'd wake up with a major case of bad hair and breath strong enough to dissolve nail polish.

Jake was setting the table when Jilly and I came in. We locked eyes for a long time. He walked over and gave me a quick kiss and a whispered compliment.

During dinner, Jake didn't let go of my hand.

Jilly and Lyle smiled and winked when they thought he wasn't paying attention. Jake seemed oblivious to their kidding and to the broad hints I dropped about Jilly's dad's absence. I'd been thinking about this night for, like, forever.

Jake seemed to have no more on his mind than his steak. Of course, that was to be expected, since he didn't exactly know what I had in mind for the evening. My palms sweated—what if he wasn't interested?

After dinner, we sat on the front porch. Jake and I claimed

the swing. Jilly and Lyle promptly entwined on the big wicker couch. We were in time to catch the last minutes of sunset. The sky turned so many colors that it made my throat ache.

Lyle went inside and came back with a couple of beers and another bottle of wine. The lightning bugs flashed their hellos to the night. I remembered how Jilly and I used to chase them in the dark.

After a couple of swigs of her wine, Jilly jumped up. "What do you want to do now?" She couldn't sit still for more than two seconds. I think she was nervous for me. Lyle grabbed her and tickled her.

Jake took my hand and pulled me up. "May I have this dance?"

"Here?" I felt a little foolish, dancing on the front porch.

"Sure, why not?"

"I'll put on some music." Jilly jumped up. A minute later, something slow and sultry came out of the overhead sound system.

Jake held out his arms and I went into them. Into him. I felt like we were pouring into each other through our skin. His fingers were warm as he smoothed my back through the fabric of my dress.

We danced to song after song as night wrapped around us like a cocoon. I barely noticed when Jilly and Lyle called out a quiet good night. I was dizzy from the wine and the feel of Jake's body against mine. We were pressed tight like we had melted together. I kept thinking he would kiss me, but he didn't.

His hands moved over me like restless butterflies, skimming the surface, but never landing in one spot. I nuzzled his neck, just a little, but his reaction wasn't exactly what I expected. He jumped as if electrified, then abruptly stopped dancing.

"Want a soda or something? We polished off two bottles of wine."

"Sure." Why was Jake trying to sober me up? I'd only had a few glasses of wine.

I stood there for a second, blinking. It was like someone had turned on floodlights in a candlelit room.

Jake tugged on my hand and I followed him to the basement bar, where he poured me a soda. Then he sat next to me on the sofa to watch me drink it.

"Megan, are you sure? About—us, I mean."

"I'm sure, Jake. I'm finally sure."

Then he kissed me, with a new, meaningful question on his tongue. I answered with my whole body and soul. There was no hesitation.

I was glad Jilly had stocked my room with enough birth control for a sex ed class. I had a feeling I was going to need it. And I was right.

* * *

The next morning, lemon pudding sunshine poured over the bed. It felt weird to wake up next to someone. Not just someone, but Jake. We were snuggled together like two spoons.

But in the bright light of day, *naked* is a whole different ball game.

Let's not even talk about my embarrassment at the idea of a guy seeing my breasts in daylight. I didn't know where to look. I mean, there was a nude guy in my bed. Not exactly an everyday occurrence. At least not for me.

Then, for some reason I couldn't really explain, I had a vision of him morphing into a Peter clone. Talking to his buddies about the size of my breasts, the little noises I made when—I stopped right at that thought. Not like Jake at all.

I took a deep breath. Jake wasn't Peter, and I shouldn't worry.

Jake brushed the hair back from my face. "Megan, are you okay?"

I desperately wanted to brush my teeth. I wanted to put on my flannel jammies, the ones with the hole in the knee. Heck, right now, I'd trade a night's worth of tips for a breath mint.

To make matters worse, the sheet, which I had pulled up to my chin when I woke up, was slipping. I grabbed a corner and held on for dear life. I'd try to distract Jake and get dressed while he wasn't peeking. Yeah, right, like *that* was gonna happen.

I know, I know. Yes, he saw me naked last night. It seemed

like a great idea at the time. But now I didn't like the idea, not one bit. I didn't want him to see me without my clothes, and I definitely didn't want him to touch me. I just wanted him out of the room. Here's this great guy, someone I've had a major crush on for years, and I've just had sex with him. And all I want to do is take a shower. Alone. *Confused* doesn't even begin to cover it.

"Don't you have to work this morning?" I checked the clock on the nightstand. "It's already after six."

"Damn, you're right." He jumped from the bed and went searching for his clothes.

I secretly admired Jake's nude body as he scooped up a sock here, his underwear there. It was pretty evident from the clothes strewn all over the room that I had been pretty sure of something the night before.

Now my emotions jumbled together like the stuff in my mom's junk drawer. Jake tossed on his clothes and grabbed his keys. Not my idea of a romantic good-bye, I thought. But before he left, he came to where I lay with the sheet up to my neck.

He kissed me—a long, slow kiss. A kiss like he didn't have to be at work in less than fifteen minutes. My morning breath and crazy hair didn't seem to bother him at all. Then he said, "I gotta go. I'll come over after work, okay? I love you, Megan."

He left before I could stutter out a *"what did you say?"*

Chapter

16

Mrs. Westland, after Jake raced off to work, I flipped his "I love you" over and over, but the words wouldn't seem to take shape. Instead, the words turned my brain to goop.

My body pulsed with energy, but at the same time, I was strangely lethargic. I stripped the bed and threw the sheets into the wash. But I couldn't wash away what had happened the night before.

My brain was still processing the fact that I'd finally let someone see me, all of me. Although Jake was so much more than just a "someone."

After taking a quick shower and throwing on my favorite vegging-out clothes, I left a note for Jilly and walked the few blocks to my house. Nobody was home. I left a "just checking in" note for my mom and grabbed a couple of magazines on the way out the door. It was more out of habit than anything else. I didn't really feel like snipping out pictures.

One way to take my mind off Jake was to fret about someone else. Susi Fielding's face popped into my mind. I know Jake thought that it was none of our business, and it probably wasn't. But even though Susi went in backseats as often as I served pancakes, I thought she was in over her head this time. It wasn't like Mr. C. could take her to the senior prom or anything, even if he weren't married.

I crossed the street and rang the doorbell at Susi's. How was I going to let Susi know I cared, without sounding like a Butterball busybody? Besides, the last time I'd tried to help, Susi told me to butt out. No answer. Maybe Jake was right and I should just stay out of it.

As I turned to leave, Susi's mom opened the door. "Megan—nice to see you." She was underwhelmed.

I'd never seen Mrs. Fielding without makeup. Her bare face gave her a weary beauty I'd never seen before. I'd never noticed that underneath the makeup, she appeared young enough to be Susi's sister.

"Hi, Mrs. Fielding. May I please speak to Susi?"

"She's not here right now." Without warning, Susi's mom started crying. "She hasn't been home all night and hasn't called. Susi's a little wild, but she's never done that before, not ever."

Should I tell her about what I saw at the Palace? I could just imagine Susi's reaction to that little chat. Not to mention that Susi's mom was way too freaked out to hear her daughter was having an affair with her boss.

I was feebly patting her back when Steve Hanover pulled up in his squad car. What was he doing here? I figured it out when Mrs. Fielding brushed by me and went running to the car. I followed.

"Did you find her?"

"No, Karen, I didn't. It'll be a few more hours before I can put an APB out."

"Damn it, Steve, I want to know where my daughter is. She's never done this before."

"Try . . ." I spoke without thinking, and trailed off as two pairs of eyes skewered me where I stood.

"Megan, do you know something? If you do, you've got to tell us!" Mrs. Fielding ended with a semi-hysterical shriek.

I stood there, mind racing. Susi would probably never talk to me anyway, and she needed help. I couldn't bear her mom's pain.

"Check for Mr. Cooper's car. She may be with him." It was a relief to tell. It was a relief until I saw Susi's mom's face. I told Mrs. Fielding what I knew, leaving out the basement scene. I knew Susi would never forgive me if her mom knew about that.

I didn't have to worry, though. When Steve came back with Susi, it was fairly obvious where she'd been. Susi had two glowing hickeys on her neck, which provided a small hint.

When she saw Susi, Mrs. Fielding gave a sob of relief, followed by a string of curses. She used words I'd only heard coming out of Dennis's mouth, never a grown-up's. Susi's mom marched over to the squad car and pulled her daughter out. I stiffened, ready to come to Susi's defense, but Mrs. Fielding only hugged her tight, scolding her the whole time.

"Where was she, Steve?" Mrs. Fielding demanded.

Susi pulled away from her mom and walked over to me. I could see the tears in her eyes, but she glared at me—right before she slapped my face and walked into the house, without saying a word.

Steve glanced at me standing on the front porch and lowered his voice. ". . . found her with him at the Motel 6 out by the state line." I strained to hear. "Do you want to press charges? He's at the station right now, answering some questions."

"Do I want to press charges? What kind of asinine question is that!" Susi's mom was shouting. The whole town could probably hear. "Of course I want to press charges. I want that pervert Mr. Cooper put away, the longer the better. Need I remind you my daughter's a minor?"

Steve mumbled something about Mr. Cooper's family, but he seemed resigned to making an arrest, something he probably hadn't had to do in Fairview for some time.

I wished Mrs. Fielding had been there when the town cops

went to talk to Peter after he groped me. She wouldn't have let him get off with a warning.

Jilly was sunbathing by the pool when I got to her house.

"Jake called, like, five times, Megan." I didn't say anything.

"So give. I want details." Jilly stared at me. "Funny, you don't look any different."

"Total myth. Jilly, it's too new. I'm not ready to talk about it yet." For some reason, I didn't want to fill her in on every detail of my night with Jake.

"Let's go see Jake at work. I have major news about Mr. Cooper. I'll fill you in on the way."

We went by my house so I could change into something a little more attractive. Jilly was practically coming unglued by the suspense, but I didn't say anything until we were in her car on the way to Pancake Palace.

"Mr. Cooper got arrested," I announced.

"Yay!" Jilly screamed with glee.

"He deserved it, whatever it was," she added.

"I'm the one who told Susi's mom. Susi's really pissed off at me."

"Megan, Susi was in way over her head. I think you did the right thing, but do you think so?"

I nodded, and then said, "But sometimes doing the right thing doesn't feel so great."

The rest of the ride was quiet. I wondered if I had done the right thing with Jake and me. Somehow, I doubted it. I couldn't be that lucky. And he was due to leave for college in less than a week.

When we got to the Palace, the place was in an uproar. Everyone in town had already heard the news of Mr. Cooper's arrest and headed to Pancake Palace to hash it out at the scene of the crime, so to speak. The restaurant was wall-to-wall with gossipers.

I saw Jake's back as he flipped burgers in the kitchen, and suddenly, I was warm all over, like I'd been standing a little too close to the grill.

Mrs. Stevens, the assistant manager, bustled up. "Girls, I know you're both off today, but would you mind helping out for an hour or so? People are coming out of the woodwork since they've heard about—well, I could use the help."

"Sure, Mrs. Stevens."

"Don't worry about changing. Just punch in. Jilly, you can man the counter. Megan, can you set up the salad bar? Thanks!"

While I got out the potato salad, I worried about how Jake would act now that we'd been together. I remembered the way he nuzzled my neck the last time I had salad bar duty. I may be the only person in this world to find a salad bar sexy.

Jake didn't disappoint me. He came to the back kitchen about a minute after I did. As he wrapped his arms around me and whispered in my ear, my uncertainty disappeared. At least for those few minutes. I would deal with my doubts later. Unfortunately, later came sooner than I expected.

Chapter 17

Mrs. Westland, Mr. Cooper was all anyone could talk about at the Palace. Mr. Cooper and "some young girl," but Susi's name was never mentioned, at least not out loud. The whole restaurant was gossiping so much that it's a miracle we didn't screw up all the orders.

We got a new manager at the Palace right away. Mrs. Stevens, the assistant manager who worked mostly days, was promoted. I bet Mr. Henderson figured the teen help was safe from her.

Susi and I worked a couple shifts together. She wouldn't say one word to me, but Jilly told me Susi and her mom were in therapy. It was a start.

Speaking of moms, I didn't know it, but my mom had planned our school shopping trip. It was weird being alone with her, since I couldn't remember the last time we'd hung out without Dad or at least one set of twins.

The trip didn't start out very well. When I came home from

taking my chemistry final, Mom was waiting for me. She met me at the door.

"Megan, I've made the reservations for this weekend. We can leave early Saturday morning." I hadn't seen my mom this excited since she won the big money at bingo.

"Reservations?" I said.

"Our overnight trip, remember? Just the two of us. You said after finals."

I'd completely forgotten.

"But Jake leaves for college in a few days." As soon as the words left my mouth, I knew I'd said the wrong thing.

Her shoulders stiffened. "Maybe we should just skip it, since you can't make time for me this once."

Boy, look who was talking. I couldn't remember the last time my mom had time for me, at least time that didn't involve a lecture. But I knew better than to say anything. Besides, it occurred to me that I was in danger of becoming one of those girls I despised, a girl who planned her entire existence around her boyfriend's schedule.

"I want to go, really. But I have to get someone to cover my shifts."

"Done. I called Mrs. Stevens already."

Part of me hated how she'd simply rearranged my life without telling me, but part of me was glad I'd have my mom all to myself. Still, I wasn't sure what we'd talk about on the three-hour drive to Minneapolis.

I'd said good-bye to Jake the night before. It was a bit of a sore subject that I was going on this trip with my mom. Our good-bye involved long kisses, but no condom-worthy contact. Who knows what would have happened if Jake hadn't been pouting. Not even Jake Darrow can make pouting seem attractive.

I hadn't asked what he'd be doing over the weekend. I was still dealing with the new knowledge that Jake wasn't perfect. He was too used to getting his own way.

I hadn't asked what Jake would be doing, but I hoped it wouldn't involve his ex. Savannah was still in town. I wasn't worried, not exactly.

Dad and the little guys got up early to see us off Saturday morning. David and Dennis were nowhere to be seen, probably still in bed, recovering from some leaving-for-college binge. Mom let me drive the first hour of the trip. We stopped for coffee and donuts, sang along with the radio, and generally had a great time. Until it was time to shop for clothes.

We finally got to the Mall of America in Bloomington, just outside Minneapolis. The Mall of America is part shopping mall, part tourist attraction, and part theme park. It's also huge, maybe the biggest mall in the U.S. When Mom mentioned shopping, I was thinking a quick trip to Old Navy or something, and then exploring Minneapolis. Mom had marathon shopping in mind.

I groaned, just a little, as we pulled into the parking lot. Mom shot me a sharp glance but didn't say anything.

I didn't like shopping for clothes, not really. Everything makes my chest look bigger, except my usual baggy shirts and pants, which (I hoped) made me look like I didn't have a shape at all.

The shops blurred, one into another. My feet were swollen, and I could tell Mom was frustrated. We finally ended up at a funky little boutique with surprisingly reasonable prices. Mom held up a sweater about three sizes smaller than the ones I usually wear.

"That would be great on her," a salesclerk said. She was drop-dead gorgeous. I couldn't help but notice she wasn't exactly lacking in the breast department herself, and yet she wore a tiny sweater with one button left unbuttoned at the bottom to show off her perfectly flat stomach. She was curvy, in a Pamela-Anderson-without-the-silicone kind of way. Her name tag read "Gina."

Mom must have agreed with Gina, because she grabbed the sweater in three colors and herded me toward the changing room. She stopped long enough to ask, "Do you carry jeans?"

"Sure. What about a pair like these?" Gina said in her best sales voice.

I gulped. She wore a pair of reveal-every-curve jeans, cut like they'd been made just for her.

"Your daughter is about my size," she said to my mom.

Her size? I gulped again. I preferred jeans I could swim in.

I don't know why, but I had a "why not?" moment, and allowed Gina and my mom to convince me to try on a pair of the jeans.

I shut the door firmly in the face of my eager audience and pulled on the jeans without looking in the mirror.

I shrugged out of my shirt. I made a note that I could use a new bra. That old one needed to be retired.

Time for the sweater. I grabbed the green one and put it on, still avoiding my reflection. I took a deep breath and faced the mirror. I looked okay, better than okay.

"Mom, can you get me another green sweater one size bigger?" I called over the door. Hey, I couldn't change overnight, now could I?

I switched the sweaters and came out to model the clothes. The sweater was comfortable, but not my usual baggy shirt. My mom and Gina oohed and ahhed.

As she rang up our purchases, Gina said brightly, "Sometimes it helps to take a chance. It will make all the difference in your wardrobe."

I walked out of the boutique with three pairs of jeans, some tops, and the green sweater.

"I don't know why you don't wear clothes that fit you right more often," my mother said as we strolled the mall, trying to find a place to eat.

"Don't you?" I said. I thought it was the perfect opportunity to mention the breast reduction. I had her undivided attention.

"Don't I what?"

"Don't you know why I don't wear anything formfitting?"

She shook her head. "Why don't you tell me, honey," she said softly.

I saw an empty bench and steered my mother toward it. "I'm glad you asked. There's something I've been wanting to talk to you about," I said. And that's how I finally broke it to my mom that I wanted breast-reduction surgery.

She was surprised, but after I calmly told her a little bit of what I'd been going through, she said she'd talk to Dad. I had to agree to wait until I was in college to make my decision, but Mom said she'd find out if our insurance would cover the breast-reduction surgery. It was more than I expected.

We made a quick stop for bras and undies. Since I usually shopped for bras with Jilly, my mother was amazed at the amount of Lycra needed for a D-cup bra. We had dinner and then headed for the hotel, where we made a trip to the Jacuzzi and then collapsed. We did some sightseeing on Sunday before we headed home.

Mom had decided to drive straight through on the way back. I knew she missed Dillon and Dakota, but I could barely get her to stop for restroom breaks. The rest of our trip passed without any further confessions, and we made it home, tired and cranky.

Dennis and David were in the living room, watching

television, when we walked in. Mom headed upstairs to see the little guys.

"Hey, what's up?" I threw myself on the couch. "Did Jake call?"

"Nope." Dennis stared at the TV.

"What did you guys do this weekend?" I said, to make conversation. Believe me, I was not hoping for explicit details.

"We went to a party," David said. "It was . . . ," he trailed off, looking uncertainly at Dennis.

I was immediately suspicious. "What was it, David?" I said, trying to sound like I didn't care. Something was up. My brothers never hesitated to fill me in on the gory details of their parties.

"You guys may as well tell me before Butterball does," I said, my stomach full of knots.

"It's no big deal, Megan. It's just that Savannah and Jake were both at the party, and they—" Dennis said.

I knew it. Fury fogged my brain. Tears pooled at the corner of my eyes, but I refused to let them fall.

"Hey, Sis, I was just kidding. Jake didn't even go to the party," Dennis said. He sounded sincere. I wanted to believe him.

"Savannah was all over Kevin. Honest. Megan, don't worry, all Jake did was wait for you all weekend," Dennis added.

I took a shaky breath, still near tears.

"Yeah, he's whipped all right," Dennis said, and stood to give me a hug. "We were just messin' with you. Sorry."

I believed my brothers. Honestly. But it did bring up an interesting question. What would Jake do when he was thousands of miles away? He couldn't spend every weekend in his dorm room, as tempting as that idea sounded to me. I pushed the problem out of my mind, resolving to deal with it later.

Jake and I had several unbelievable days and nights before the beginning of the end came. But it was bound to end. We tried to avoid the unavoidable: Jake's departure.

I was so sure that we belonged together when he held me in his arms. But on those rare nights I was alone, I'd sit outside in the hammock and stare at the stars. I pictured Jake's plane, the plane he would leave me on, passing under those same stars.

I couldn't really see a relationship as new as ours withstanding a few thousand miles between us. Not to mention all the college temptations. The ones Dennis and David had been very vocally anticipating the last few days.

There was only one thing to do. Even though I didn't want to do it, I knew breaking up was the best thing for me. And for Jake.

He didn't see it that way.

We had my house to ourselves when I brought it up. "Jake, please, can't you see we have to? We're going to be apart for months at a time. When will we see each other again? Thanksgiving? Christmas?"

He shook his head, stony-faced. "It doesn't matter how long, Megan. I want you, not anyone else."

"You just broke up with Savannah not that long ago. You say that you want me now, but what if you meet someone? Then what?"

"I won't." Jake sounded so sure. Why wasn't I?

"What's this really about, Megan?" It was like he could see what I was thinking. "Do you want to go out with someone else?"

My eyes teared. I hated hurting him. "No, not at all. It's just . . . I'm not ready."

"What do you mean, 'not ready'?"

"I'm not ready for the way I feel when I'm with you, Jake. It's too much for me right now."

I could see the sharp jab each word gave him. Jake repeated my words as if measuring the weight of each syllable.

He wouldn't look at me as he walked through the living room to the front door and out of my house. Two days later, he left for college. He called to say good-bye, but I was at work, so we couldn't really talk. He sounded like a stranger. I told myself I'd made the right decision.

Dennis and David left a few days later. Dirty socks and football helmets evaporated, just disappeared from the house. Suddenly, we had all the milk we needed in the refrigerator.

I missed them. I could almost hear Dennis telling me to quit being prissy and just call the guy already. I missed Jake a lot.

He called a week later, but I was at work. Mom wrote down his number at the dorm. I called him about five times that week, but missed him because I kept forgetting about the time difference on the West Coast. Duh.

Why did I doubt Jake? I didn't even try to make our relationship work. Not really. The first sign of trouble and I just let him go. I guess this was really my first true love and I wasn't ready for such a serious relationship. At least not yet.

But not knowing what was going on with Jake made me irritable. Not knowing what was going on with me made me weepy.

Why did I have to tell him the truth? I didn't even really know what I wanted. I missed Jake like crazy, while telling myself it was all for the best. A little voice whispered *chicken* each time I looked in the mirror.

I knew Jake had just arrived at Stanford. I told myself he was probably just busy settling in, too busy to call back maybe. But I wondered. He had been so angry. Maybe angry enough to get back together with Savannah? Or to hook up with a beautiful California girl?

One night, I sat at home, pretending to not wait by the phone. My parents were at the neighbors' playing cards. Even my parents had a better social life than I did.

I jumped when I heard a car pull up. My heart *ca-chinged* like a cash register. But it was Jilly's red convertible parked at the curb. She knocked, then opened the screen door and came in.

I sat in the dark, brooding or pouting or whatever you call it when you think something great is over, when you don't want it to be.

"Megan," she said, not even saying hello. "What's up with you?"

"I've been busy."

"Yeah, I can see." She pointed to the tissues scattered on the living room carpet, the half-eaten bag of chips, and the empty cookie tin.

"We're going out tonight. Put away the binge food and get dressed."

I stuck my chin out and stared at the wall. I didn't feel like going anywhere.

"Get up, take a shower, and let's go. Now!" Jilly never talked to me like that. I moved. "And wash your hair, for god's sake," she called after me.

I felt better after my shower. I went to the living room, towel-drying my hair as I walked. I'd changed out of my grubby sweats into a clean pair of shorts and a shirt.

Jilly ushered me out the door before my hair dried.

"At least let me put some shoes on," I protested.

"Put 'em on in the car. Let's go." This was the toughest Jilly I'd ever seen.

We hopped into her convertible and just drove. For a long time. She didn't ask any questions.

Finally, I broke the silence.

"I broke up with Jake."

"I know. He called me."

"How is he?"

Jilly said, "About as good as you are, I'd say."

"I miss him, Jilly." I practically wailed it.

"Megan, why on earth did you break up with Jake? You two are perfect for each other."

"I don't really know. Scared, maybe."

"Scared of what?"

"I don't know. Scared of losing him, I guess. I just felt— it was too much. It was overwhelming. I never thought sex would be like that."

She abruptly pulled the car to the side of the road. "What'd you think it would be like, going for ice cream?"

The question made me want to cry, but I tried to explain anyway. "I just didn't think it was going to be so intense. That it would bring us even closer. I had no idea." I broke off, wanting to cry again. "Now I can't even get ahold of Jake." My voice cracked.

"Megan, did you stop to think about how Jake is feeling? He cares about you. I know I didn't think so at first, but I do now. You just threw him away. You didn't even *try* to make it work. Not for very long anyway."

Her voice softened. "It doesn't matter if you two get back together or not. You've made love. There will always be a little part of Jake Darrow with you now, whether you want it or not."

I thought about what she'd said. I'd always have a connection to Jake, even if we never saw each other again. The thought made me feel better. Despite everything that had happened this summer, I knew now I'd be okay, if I was with Jake or not.

When Jilly dropped me off, I called Jake and finally got through to him. Things still weren't the greatest between us, but at least we were talking. I hadn't totally blown it with him.

You never know—by next summer, I may be ready to take a chance. Either way, I know what it's like now to give someone I love my body—and my trust.

Jake says he likes me for what I am: a pretty, smart, and funny person. Sometimes, I believe those things, too. Not because Jake says so, but because when I look in the mirror, I can see it might be true. And that's the most unexpected development of all.

In case you're wondering, Mrs. Westland, I decided not to get the boob job, at least not next year. So I guess I'll be going away to college myself.

Susi's still not really talking to me, but the other day I saw her at the Palace. She was waiting on Brent Swenson, of all people. They were smiling and laughing as she took his order. Susi actually waved to me.

I hope Mr. Cooper has learned a thing or two, though. He's serving eighteen months in jail. I've heard his wife brings him a batch of brownies and a Bible once a week. Like Jake said, love is a strange thing.

Mrs. Westland, you're probably wondering why I told you all this. Well, you asked what I did on my summer vacation.